HE BLACKED OUT INSTANTLY AND BEGAN MOVING

He searched in the bitter cold blackness, past moonlets and hints of planetary rings. And down and down, thousands and thousands of kilometers, through immense depths of hydrogen gas.

His mind was now resting on a great platform of crushed metal, surrounded by a cyclonic soup of radioactive particles. A decade of nuclear waste, just sitting there, waiting.

He blew his mind through a few layers of plutonium two thirty-nine. The neutrons spun out like frightened sparrows, then settled into illusory safety in neighboring atoms—which began breaking up. Critical mass was on the way, and when it came, fission would be total: one hundred percent. He had to get out. Quickly.

Other Avon Books by
Charles L. Harness

KRONO
LURID DREAMS

LUNAR JUSTICE

CHARLES L. HARNESS

AVON BOOKS ◆ NEW YORK

The author gratefully acknowledges William D. Barney's permission to quote from his poem "The Hill Hounds." This poem previously appeared in Mr. Barney's collection *Kneel From the Stone* (Dallas, TX.: Kalleidograph Press, 1952) and *Quicksilver* Magazine.

LUNAR JUSTICE is an original publication of Avon Books. This work has never before appeared in book form. This work is a novel. Any similarity to actual persons or events is purely coincidental.

AVON BOOKS
A division of
The Hearst Corporation
1350 Avenue of the Americas
New York, New York 10019

Copyright © 1991 by Charles L. Harness
Cover art by Glen Orbik
Published by arrangement with the author
Library of Congress Catalog Card Number: 91-91788
ISBN: 0-380-76010-X

First Avon Books Printing: August 1991

AVON TRADEMARK REG. U.S. PAT. OFF. AND IN OTHER COUNTRIES, MARCA REGISTRADA, HECHO EN U.S.A.

Printed in the U.S.A.

RA 10 9 8 7 6 5 4 3 2 1

To Daisy Nell,
my dearest friend

The hill hounds, furious for the fox,
rive their red throats, deep horns of hell,
a flame of sound, a fire of fear,
and the grey fox crouching knows them well.

For the blanched moon pitiless is poured
white on the hills, a gaunt slow glare;
the fear goes far, and the grey fox hears
and the moaning combs his prickling hair.

—William D. Barney,
   from "The Hill Hounds"

I
Nadys

Ah, Moon of my Delight
Who know'st no wane.
         —The Rubáiyát of Omar Khayyám

He was sitting in the recreation room with Nadys and half a dozen of her companion guests, and they were chatting idly as they watched the morning news on the holo. It was that crazy Lamplighter Project again. Quentin Thomas didn't give it his full attention. He was studying his beloved from the corner of his eye. She had now been here at the resort a full week, and it still didn't make any sense to him. She had tried to explain at the beginning of the retreat: "Listen to me, darling. With a man, marriage is a simple thing, saying some words, signing some papers, off to work in the morning, home at night, eating, sleeping, sex, in one head and out the other. With a woman, though, it's a serious business. Marriage can really mess up a woman's mind. It's not a one-night stand. It's not a weekend at a resort. It's not a relationship. Quentin, sweetheart, I've got to think it through. I need peace and quiet. I need a week here at Patuxent Haven. Maybe two weeks."

So he had sighed, and he had tried to look at it from her viewpoint. He could see that to live with him and to give up certain freedoms, to rearrange her entire life, would require some deep and time-consuming soul-searching. Well, he could wait. He compared it to the task of netting a beautiful and very wary butterfly. It was a question of patience, persistence, never losing sight of the quarry, never making any sudden moves. Eventually he was going to

1

persuade this remarkable girl to marry him. It was just a question of time.

"Look!" she commanded.

Back to the holo. The announcer, a diminutive ten-inch three-D figure, was demonstrating something with models on a table. From time to time the cameras zoomed in on a particular object to make a point. "This," said the announcer, "is a model of the planet Jupiter. Note the light and dark bands. Here's the GRS—the Great Red Spot, a cloud storm that's been whirling for thousands, maybe millions of years. Over the last ten years the Lamplighters have dumped millions of tons of nuclear waste into the GRS. They claim there's now enough waste at the planet core to ignite Jupiter—turn it into a small second sun. And *that* would warm up its moons and make them habitable. However—"

Cut to file tape. Announcer's voiceover: "Michael Dore—the driving force behind the Lamplighters." A tall gray-haired man held a model of something in his hand, a sort of metallic capsule. Quentin Thomas caught some explanation. "This is the fuse that will start the nuclear reaction at Jupiter's core. We shoot it into the GRS. It falls through thousands of kilometers of hydrogen and helium gases, then through a shell of liquid helium, and finally it arrives at the solid core, and there it searches out our pile of waste. And then—bang. The fuse blows, the waste blows, the planet starts fusing hydrogen, and Jupiter becomes a titanic hydrogen fusion bomb . . ." The voice faded. The announcer again: "That was two months ago. What went wrong? Nobody knows. But Mr. Dore was not daunted by failure. He promised to try again. His next attempt was supposed to involve something ultra-secret. The secret didn't stay secret very long. The story that reached us was that Mr. Dore hired a psi to ignite the nuclear pile. He was supposed to set it off by brain waves. We traced the leak back to the psi himself, a Professor Siva. Dr. Siva was supposed to increase his power with the aid of a little black box—a psi-enhancer invented by Mr. Dore. However, the professor was never given a chance to show what he could do, because he vanished, along with the psi-enhancer, soon after the story broke. So where does this leave the great Lamplighter Project? Nobody knows for sure. We have not been able to reach Mr. Dore. In fact, he too seems to have vanished. Is he in trouble? We think so. Five years ago he promised that he would ignite Jupiter by five o'clock July 27 of this year—and that's next week. Meanwhile, he has accepted billions from a number of Federation governments. Is Michael Dore the biggest fraud of the century, or is he just an airy-brained philanthropist whose pet charity went haywire?''

There was more, but Thomas was rising from his chair. He smiled at Nadys. "I have to be going."

"A client?"

He looked casually about the big room. "Yeah, Penal Systems."

For the past minute or two he had felt that something here was slightly awry. He sensed that the blue drapes lining the picture window were actually closed-circuit pickups. He was being recorded. Interesting, but not surprising. Peace Eternal boasted tight security for the guests of its resorts. Fair enough. Out of curiosity he reached out with his mind and traced the circuitry back into a central data bank. There were a couple of coded traps, which he eluded easily. And so into Nadys's file dossier. It had complete information about her. Age, marital status, how much she made as an examiner in the Patent Office. Relatives, friends, visitors. Very thorough. (Just a bit *too* thorough?) And there was a short paragraph on him, with a couple of kine-shots. Quentin Thomas, fiancé (?) . . . age . . . physical description . . . eyes, chestnut hazel . . . hair, brown . . . height, five-nine . . . weight, one hundred fifty . . . occupation, lawyer . . .

Like Narcissus, he watched the data's mirroring flow. He resisted a temptation to straighten his tie.

Bump! Something had just been added to Nadys's data bank. Back up, Quentin. Ah . . . "*T—July 27.*" Hmm. That was early next week, the day before she was scheduled to leave. And just exactly what did "T" mean? None of his business, really.

He looked around at the group and noted a couple of empty chairs. "You say goodbye to Mrs. Casio for me."

"Oh dear. I meant to mention . . . she passed away yesterday. Very strange. She seemed in good health, excellent spirits. A cardiac, they said."

"Oh." He didn't know what to say. He hesitated. "Well, tell Mr. McCormack hello."

She shook her head. "Him, too." She shrugged. "Stroke. Very sudden. Surprised us all. He was over eighty, though."

He essayed a smile. "Just don't let it happen to *you*." ("T"—?)

She laughed her miniature chirping laugh. "Don't be silly."

They embraced and kissed, almost shyly. The odor of flowers rose up from her and engulfed him. A couple of the older women watched them hungrily. (Ah, Nadys, he thought, just you wait.) He ran his fingers through her long black hair, then caressed her scalp with his fingertips. Strange hair. Truly black, yet it had hints of gold, especially when the light was just right. She blamed that on her maternal grandfather, a redheaded Irishman. Gorgeous, he mused, and he wondered if it was Mendelian and whether their children would inherit it or any of her beauty. Of course they would. But would they inherit her natural perfume? No, that wasn't Mendelian. He would not share that with their children. He took a deep breath. That was for him alone. Not even Nadys could detect it; she was not aware of her own perfume.

She was talking to him. *"Practice,"* she whispered. "Practice your patent claims. *Rhythm!* Don't forget."

It took him a moment to get back to earth. "Patent claims . . . rhythm . . . practice . . . no, I won't forget." Rhythm. The new buzzword in the Patent Office.

He winked across Nadys's head at one of the more interested lady guests. She winked back, unabashed, and didn't turn away. She had been there, he thought.

He considered Nadys's final instructions. Practice claim rhythm. (A *truth* drug *char*acterized . . . no, no. The meter was non-homogeneous. No matter, he'd work on it back in Arlington. "I'll practice," he promised.

She pushed him away. "Enough. Go."

As he was leaving he caught the closing words of the holo commercial. ". . . brought to you by Peace Eternal, where you can rest in carefree dignity . . ."

He frowned. T—July 27. They were taking good care of her here. So why should he suddenly feel uneasy? Should he stop by the front desk and ask the receptionist what "T—July 27" meant? Not sure that would be a good idea. How could he explain where he had seen the entry? Tell them he was a psi? That would hardly do. Anyhow, he had to move along. He had a luncheon date with a valuable client.

He walked to his car in a bemused reverie. Curious, he thought, she was here, trying to figure out how it would be, living with him, for better or worse, all that stuff, day after day, month after month, year after year. With her, it wasn't just a question of sharing his bed. She'd be giving up small treasured liberties that he would probably never be able to name. For her, everything would change. Ever since college she had lived her own life, paid her own way, dealt with challenges and obstacles all by herself, and had thereby achieved a remarkable independence of mind and spirit. Apparently she felt that all of this would be at risk.

How about the other side of the coin? How about *him*? *He* did not have any problems at all in visualizing what their married life would be like. He knew it would be good. He had absolutely no doubts about that. He loved to be with her, he loved just to have her within visible, oral, audible, tactile range. He loved to talk to her, discuss things with her. She was a good listener. They thought the same things were funny, and they loved to laugh together. When she wasn't around, he missed her. Sometimes he actually ached for want of her.

He could not list all his feelings for her. The list would be endless, and would finally trail off into mystery.

But he could sum it up in four little words, which he now whispered: "Nadys, I love you."

He was astonished to find that he was standing beside his car. Enough! Back into the world! He shook his head and blinked vigorously. He had to start thinking about his patent cases.

As he drove he listened to the continuing newscast. Michael Dore was reported to be in hiding on the moon. Michael Dore was in imminent danger of arrest and trial. Mediamen by the dozen were overbidding for space on the shuttle. Moving in for the kill. Some already in Lunaplex, on hot tips developed days ago. (Thomas yawned. Who cares?) Also, the police had found Dr. Siva, the Lamplighters' psi. Dr. Siva was in a private mental institution. (Quentin Thomas started paying close attention.) The psychic was reported to be totally catatonic. He had even lost his knee-jerk and pupillary reflexes. Nobody at the sanatorium would talk, but a medical consultant for the station opined that Dr. Siva's mind had been destroyed by massive psychic stress—possibly by exposure to the Lamplighters' psi-enhancer—if indeed there were any such machine.

Thomas frowned. All this stuff about psi and its dangers was making him nervous. But why should it? None of his affair.

As he was turning into Penal Systems' parking lot, he caught a flash from a distant hill. A sun reflection. A window glass? No, too small. A camera lens, more likely. Was there an automatic camera out there focused on all the comings and goings to Penal Systems? Nonsense. This was a combination of paranoia and a low blood sugar level brought on by a skimpy breakfast. He hoped that lunch would not be long delayed.

2
"Do You Have a Daemon?"

Everyone is a moon, and has a dark side which he never shows to anybody.
    —Mark Twain

Always in the past when Penal Systems Inc. wanted to consult Quentin Thomas about an invention, they had sent someone to talk to him in his little office at Laurence, Gottlieb, in Arlington, Virginia. This time, though, they had asked him to talk to them at their place in nearby Maryland. "Can you make it about one o'clock?" the receptionist had asked. "Mr. Wright would like to have lunch with you."

That was fine with him. It was always a good idea to know as much about a client as possible, not to mention that it gave him a chance to visit Nadys. And so he had welcomed the fast drive into the heart of the Washington-Baltimore bedroom communities, capped by the winding tree-lined roads of the industrial park in Oldcolumbia.

And now here he was in the office of the administrator, the man who authorized patent work and who paid the bills: J. Henry Wright.

Wright studied him, and he studied Wright. The administrator seemed deliberately nondescript. His face was pale, wrinkled; he was of average height. In strange contrast to a pink puffy neck, his lips were thin, bloodless. When the two men shook hands Thomas noted the palm was smooth and soft, but dry.

Wright indicated the empty chair; they both sat down.

7

So far neither had said a word. It was as though time had ceased for the older man.

Thomas shrugged mentally and looked around the office. The room was conventionally arranged. Elegant carpet, mahogany furniture, genuine oils on the walls. Flowers in a corner planter. Twin mirror panels behind Wright's desk. And one of those mirrors—

Fascinating . . .

Very delicately he let the psychic tentacles of his mind probe beyond the mirror. Yes, something was there; a closed-circuit camera. He quickly traced the electronics. He was being broadcast to a distant receiver. A very, very distant receiver. How far? He couldn't quite make it out. The . . . *moon?*

Did Wright know? Of course Wright knew. His host was watching him carefully. Did Wright know that he, Quentin Thomas, could see through that mirror, and beyond? Quite possibly.

And now, finally, Wright spoke. He said, "Do you have a demon?" The intonation was smooth, modulated. The administrator might have been asking the lawyer whether he had had a nice drive out, or how the weather was back in Virginia.

A demon? thought Thomas. Do I have a demon?

What's going on here?

What had started as a routine client contact was turning into a very serious problem. Perhaps even a deadly problem. Should he demand an explanation? Well, not right away. That could make things even worse.

Demon?

In his mind he listened to the question again.

Ah! There. Not demon. *Daemon.* The meanings were entirely different. Daemons were creatures in Greek mythology ranking somewhere between gods and men. Wright was asking him, Do you have a godlike inner spirit? Do you have a talent beyond the range of common human experience? Well, maybe.

He remembered the furor when the Georgetown medics had installed his standard cranial microchips and ear sockets. All law students had to get the core chip (Nine Thousand

Rules and Cases—NTRC, or Enturc, as it was called.) The
surgery was outpatient, harmless, painless. Ordinarily it was
about as exciting as getting a haircut.

The medics had given him his standard installations, but
they had made a big fuss about it. The program supervisor
called in two outside cerebralists, and they had let him look
and listen as they talked about him. The four of them had
looked at the plates together.

Supervisor: Here we're in the auditory/speech area. Those
    fuzzy things that look like sea urchins are neurons. The
    hairs are dendrites, and they are vibrating.
First outsider: That's quite impossible. Dendrites don't
    move. They make contact via neurotransmitters. Does
    he dispense with chemical neurotransmitters?
Supervisor: Not at all! He's got all the standards: adren-
    aline, noradrenaline, dopamine, serotonin, enkaphalin,
    dynorphin, P, GABA, glutamic acid, plus at least half
    a dozen new ones. To further complicate the picture,
    he has three new brain waves, all with frequencies
    faster than the traditional beta, which gallops along at
    better than fourteen cycles per second.

(He remembered not liking standing there while they
talked about him as though he were some rare, abnormal
medical curiosity. So he had broken in, a bit truculently.)

Thomas: What's *that*? (Pointing.)
Second outsider: (Answering, but in a way that ignored
    the questioner.) That's the corpus callosum. Ordinarily
    it consists of some two hundred million fibers con-
    necting the right and left hemispheres. He has at least
    double that; maybe as much as a billion. The connec-
    tions encourage the two brain halves to talk to each
    other; the fibers provide a lot of cybernetic feedback.
    He's got more connectors than the worldwide tele-
    phone-radio network.
Supervisor: (Showing them another plate.) You'll note
    he has several extra sulci. They effectively double the
    cortical area of his frontal lobes.

First outsider: This could rank with the discovery of the aquifer on the Sioux Reservation by—what was the name of that Indian? Yes, John Running Deer.

Second outsider: Just another dowser.

(They had forgotten all about him. They were arguing.)

First outsider: This was different. The aquifer is active only when Running Deer is nearby. When it runs, the volume is tremendous—three times that of the Colorado River at flood. Also, the flow originates in a totally dry stratum. The inference is that he's taking it from Lake Agassiz, which dried up soon after the last ice age. Dissolved carbon dioxide dates the water to eighteen thousand years B.C.E.

Second outsider: Obviously, gross error—errors—somewhere.

First outsider: Oh, really? Then how do you account for that native girl in Johannesburg? She walks through the countryside and picks up rough diamonds. She has been arrested. And that boy in Fukien Province, China, who can make rain fall on his village at will?

Second outsider: (Shaking his head politely.) With all respect, I must say these reports have no scientific basis.

First outsider: Well, then, how about Monsieur Gamma, in a prison in Paris? From his cell he publishes a monthly prediction of disasters—floods, earthquakes, fires, train wrecks, space catastrophes. He's right ninety percent of the time. He caught that Denver nuclear meltdown.

Second outsider: So did forty others. You didn't need psi to see *that* one coming.

First outsider: (To supervisor.) I'm thinking about a paper. If you'll let me borrow him for a few days.'' (As though the student Quentin Thomas were a book or an umbrella!)

But he had already decided, the hell with all this. No more tests, and no paper. That night he had stood outside the Psych Building and he had mentally screwed up all the records. Which was maybe a stupid thing to do, because that probably confirmed their worst suspicions. But they had never contacted him again, and it had all quieted down.

Until now, here in the office of J. Henry Wright. Until now, when Mr. Wright had asked him a very explosive question.

So it hadn't died. It had just been lying dormant. Somebody knew. Somebody had asked questions about him. And so now this.

A daemon? Did he have a daemon?

And if he did, or didn't, what business was it of J. Henry Wright or of Penal Systems Inc.? What was supposed to have been a simple business session was taking a strange turn! What had daemons to do with PSI?

PSI? Psi?

Psi . . . Aha! Was *that* it? Was Penal Systems Inc. an elaborate cover for a psi project? A psi project involving a patent program? Were they checking him out to see whether he could be trusted with a highly secret psi technology? But what did they mean, *daemon*?

All this went through his mind in milliseconds.

He faced the office manager and answered the question: "Yes."

The impassive Mr. Wright didn't even blink. If the answer surprised him, he didn't show it. He said simply, in a rising inflection that converted the statement into a question: "You have a bumper sticker, Mr. Thomas: 'Stop the human race, not the nuclear race.' "

"Yes." Nosy bastards; they picked that up before he came out here. Translation: This interview began days ago. They knew all the answers already. They just wanted to see what he'd say.

Wright looked at his desk clock and smiled. "Well, one o'clock . . . shall we step out for a bite?"

"Fine." Thomas rose. "I'd like to stop by . . ."

"Of course. Right down the hall."

The instant he was inside the little washroom he sensed . . . oddities. The place had evidently been installed very recently. The plumbing was new. He smelled fresh paint.

He walked over to the urinal. Again, something . . . not quite right. His mind tentacles drifted along the plumbing, into the wall . . . and there everything stopped. And the flush lever . . . it wasn't connected to any incoming water line. The whole thing had been installed simply for his sole and exclusive use. They were trying to collect an undiluted specimen of his urine. Did they think he was a drug addict? That he was ill? They were giving him a physical . . . as well as a mental. He was flattered. How to repay this over-whelming display of attention?

There must be a way. Yes. This morning, at his alleged breakfast at the fast-food joint, he had picked up a couple of extra paper packets of instant coffee and sugar. He fished these out of his pockets and emptied the contents into the urinal. Anything else? Yes, here's a couple of aspirin. And now a little soap powder. And finally their desired specimen, which will drain into their hidden collection vessel and confuse the hell out of some lab technician somewhere.

He now walked over to the lavatory to wash his hands, and here he encountered another singularity. The faucets were obviously proximity-activated. The prospective user simply waved a hand at the desired tap, hot or cold, and it turned on automatically. He waved, but nothing turned on. He explored the mechanism mentally. Here we are, a simple glitch, easily fixed. There was a microscopic patch of U-238 overhead which was supposed to release a stream of neutrons, which in turn were supposed to reflect back from the hands, and activate a circuit. But something was inter-fering with the neutron flow. Nothing was coming out of the generator. And he sensed why. The packet should have included a few U-235 atoms to start the flow. Then the stream would have been self-perpetuating. Well, he could fix that. Just a question of stripping protons from some U-238s. And there we are. That should give enough U-235s for a good stream. Zap! Both faucets now responded to the approach of hands. And for this, a small plumber's bill. He thrust a wet hand toward the towel dispenser. A paper towel rolled out. Similar proximity mechanism, and it worked nicely. But everything can be improved . . . fine-tuned. Yes, here's what we do. He probed the towel circuitry and the faucet circuitry simultaneously. He made certain intricate adjustments. Then he stood back, waited a moment, then thrust both hands at the faucet taps. No water came out; instead, the towel dispenser began cranking out segment after segment of paper. He grinned and grabbed at the cellulose cascade. It stopped instantly. Both faucets came on.

Paid in full.

He left the room with springy step.

They ate in the restaurant in the spaceport near Oldcolumbia. Over red wine and filet mignon Quentin Thomas gave his periodic summary report for pending Penal Systems patent applications.

"The seismic case . . . all claims allowed. We'll pay the final fee in due course, and the patent will issue."

"That's our earth vibration detector? To detect tunneling?"

"That's the one."

"Good. Very good. We're already granting licenses. What's next?"

"Our flame-resistant bedding case. You'll recall we had to go to the board on that. A decision is due in a week or two."

"It's just as well it's still pending," said Wright. "We think now we'd like to refile, get coverage for towels, toilet paper, even bibles. It's really quite surprising what they can set on fire."

"Fair enough." Thomas studied his notes. "We come now to Veritas, our truth drug."

"Yes. A bit of a problem there," said Wright. "As I understand it, every cross-examining attorney can require that a witness take a truth drug. Right?"

Thomas nodded agreement.

The other continued. "But the practice seems to have degenerated into a judicial laughingstock. The witness can easily neutralize sodium pentothal by taking a shot of amphetamine prior to cross-examination. When the bailiffs took to concealing the identity of the ingredients in the truth drug, spies and dark agents were able to dig out the information for a price. The underground actually printed schedules of named truth drugs and the chemicals needed to neutralize them. New, more effective veracifiers appeared, but were immediately analyzed and neutralized by the criminal elements.''

"Quite so," said Thomas. "Gamma scopalamine was countered with morpholino-amphetamine; lithium pentothal by imidazo-caffeine; ethyl-whatever by tertiary-isobutyl-whatsis. Then the broad spectrum veras, mixes of a dozen esoteric truth drugs, blasted into submission by Pananias, the criminal's great lie drug.''

"Exactly," said Wright. "Our clients complain that no known truth drug can neutralize Pananias, not even our new Veritas.''

"That's the way it used to be," admitted Thomas. "But now I think we've located the problem.''

"And what might that be?''

"The scenario goes this way: The subject takes his Pananias just before his interrogation or cross-examination. Now, let's suppose his examiners give him our Veritas, say the standard dose in water, one hundred milligrams. We know Veritas doesn't work, and now we know why: Something in the Veritas actually *catalyzes* the Pananias. If the subject takes Pananias with a Veritas chaser, he can lie all day long, elaborately and convincingly, with never a variant squiggle on the polygraph. But now we come to the oddity.''

"And what's that?''

"The peculiarity is, if he has taken Pananias, and you *don't* give him Veritas, the uncatalyzed Pananias will itself act as a truth serum.''

"Well, now, that's interesting, very interesting. But it doesn't sell any Veritas. In fact, it will probably discourage sales.''

"We aren't advertising the disadvantage," said Thomas. "In any case," he added pontifically, "the trend nowadays is to forgo truth drugs altogether. A skilled attorney considers their use a confession of incompetence. He relies on thorough preparation and pretrial discovery. When he cross-examines, he tries to know ahead of time the answers to the questions he puts to the witness. That way there's no problem with Pananias or other truth drug neutralizers.''

"But what if the attorney has no time to prepare?" asked Wright. "What if he has to take the case on an hour's notice?"

Thomas looked at the administrator with narrowing eyes. What are you driving at? he wondered. He said grimly, "I'd say both attorney and client are in deep trouble."

He waited a moment for Wright to clarify the question, but the other simply said, "I see. Too bad. Well, what else do we have?"

"That leaves the guillotine case. I interviewed that one last week. The patent examiner insists it's simple aggregation, that motorizing plus a stainless steel blade would be obvious to one skilled in the art."

"Should we appeal?"

The lawyer shook his head. "The board would affirm."

Wright sighed. "All right, let it go. But just in the U.S. The French are still interested, you know."

"We'll keep it alive in France. How about the other guillotine countries . . . Germany, Spain, Italy . . . ?"

"Yes. Go ahead with them." Wright seemed pensive.

Quentin Thomas thought, He's finally going to tell me what this is all about.

But no. Not just yet. "We have modified the guillotine," said Wright. "You might have better luck in the Patent Office with the modified machine."

"Tell me about the modification."

"Simple enough. We've added a random selection guilt avoider."

Thomas arched his eyebrows and waited.

"In our earlier model," explained Wright, "the executioner presses a button, the motor draws the blade up, it drops . . . and the executioner may or may not feel guilty about killing a fellow human being. With our new, improved model, there are three buttons, each to be pressed by a different person. An integrated computer makes a random selection as to which button actually closes the motor circuit. Nobody knows. Each of the three can say to himself—I didn't do it. And the chances are, he didn't."

"Ah. Yes, that might be patentable." Thomas was already thinking ahead. "It probably has broad applications.

Utah—computerized selection of real and blank bullets for the firing squads. Texas—random selection of which switch electrocutes the condemned man. And who drops the trap-door on the hanging scaffold, or makes the selection for the lethal injection, or releases the HCN in the gas chamber . . . macabre, Mr. Wright, but interesting.'' (And you are still hiding things from me, Mr. Wright. Important things.)

Just then Wright's wrist receiver beeped. ''Excuse me.'' He held it to his ear.

He's getting the lab report on my specimen, thought the lawyer. And maybe some choice words about what I did to their washroom. Did I go too far? Too late now.

Wright flicked off the little receiver and resumed eating. He finished his buttered carrots in silence and without making eye contact with his guest.

Thomas sipped at his coffee and waited. He had work to do this afternoon. How to get the session moving again? ''Do you want me to start work on a c-i-p to cover the random selector?'' he asked tentatively.

Wright came to life. ''Yes, eventually, I think so. But just now, we'd like for you to function in a matter of somewhat higher priority.''

''Oh?''

''Take a look out the window, Mr. Thomas.''

''The lunar freighter?''

''Yes. The nooner-lunar, I think they call it. It arrives here at noon and takes off again about three p.m. You don't see the incoming passengers. They've already gone into the re-grav rooms, where they'll learn to walk again. And then customs. You've been to the moon?''

''Yes, on vacation, a couple of years ago.''

''I've never been there myself. I understand it's an interesting place.''

''Yes. I'd like to go back someday.'' He suddenly suspected he shouldn't have said that.

''I believe they have their own judicial system,'' said the administrator.

''It's very recent. They didn't have the Lunar Court when I was there.''

''Do you know anything about it? Lunar law, I mean?''

"Just what I've read in the bar journals."

"And what might that be?"

Thomas hesitated. There were three general legal systems—common law, civil law, and lunar law. He was well aware of the reports running rife in the local bar symposia: In common law you're innocent until proven guilty; in civil law you're guilty until proven innocent; in lunar law you're guilty. But why go into that? He said finally, "Well, they have their own system. I guess you know that."

"Can any lawyer practice there? Or do you have to take a bar exam, or something?" Wright peered at him closely.

Thomas returned the look coolly. There was something very strange in these questions. He sensed that all this was familiar ground to J. Henry Wright, that the administrator (like a good cross-examiner) knew the answers before he posed the questions, and was simply evaluating Thomas's responses. The implications were confusing . . . mysterious . . . even alarming. He replied with measured calm,

"Theoretically, any lawyer admitted in a terran court can practice there. Why are you asking me all these questions, Mr. Wright?"

"Oh, no special reason, Mr. Thomas. Just curious." He looked out the window again. "Ah, it's loading now."

"Yes, I see." The baggage ramp was open, and cartons and crates of various sizes and shapes were moving up into the hold on a conveyor belt. Wright's voice rose a trifle, but not enough to suggest excitement. "See that? That black rectangular box?"

"Yes?"

"That's our guillotine, Mr. Thomas. It's headed for the moon. We are negotiating a license with the Lunar Judicial System."

The moon—so *this* was the connection. This was what it was all about. If they had only told him about this weeks, even days, ago, he could have put together a smooth, legal, risk-free patent/licensing program. But now he would have to straighten out problems he didn't understand, ask questions of people who probably knew even less than he. Oh well, might as well take it philosophically. (Quentin, Mr. Gottlieb had once explained, half of your billable hours will come from client screwups. Don't knock it.)

"They want to test it before they sign," said Wright.

"A normal business precaution."

Wright toyed with the check. "A *real* test."

Thomas thought about that. No. He couldn't mean . . .
"Excuse me?"

"There may be an execution on the moon early next
week," said Wright.

The lawyer swallowed hard. Wright *did* mean it. And
come to think of it, he had heard something . . . on the news?
Lamplighters . . . Michael Dore . . . on the moon. Something
about a capital crime. He couldn't remember. It hadn't made
much impression at the time. He took a deep breath. It was
suddenly very warm in the dining alcove.

His host continued calmly. "You are to accompany the
guillotine, Mr. Thomas. You will unpack it and assemble
it in the Rotunda at Lunaplex, for inspection and acceptance
by the chief bailiff. He will be there with some men to help
you put it together."

So that, thought Thomas, was what all the PSI patent
case chatter had been about. It was all just a delay stratagem,
just a lot of stalling, until J. Henry could get the word on
his beeper that I was to be selected for the job. But let's
slow down a bit, Mr. Wright! He said, "You mean, get on
that shuttle—*now*?"

"Well, yes."

"Wright, for God's sake! I need reservations! On the
ship, in a lunar hotel . . . and money . . . and I'll have to
check back with the firm . . . and I don't even have a change
of underwear!"

Wright replied unhurriedly, "That's all arranged, Mr.
Thomas. There's a bag, packed and waiting for you on
board. Everything in your size. And a nice room at the
Armstrong-Aldrin in Lunaplex, within walking distance of
the Rotunda. I've already talked to your partners. I believe
we've thought of everything." Wright got to his feet.

"But . . . but . . ." Thomas protested.

His host took him by the elbow and began walking him
toward exit security. And now the administrator was whispering. "Listen carefully . . . extremely important . . . set up

the machine first thing . . . as soon as you get off the ship. Then, immediately after you finish with the machine, you are to contact a person in Suite 41 at the Armstrong-Aldrin. Got that?''

''Suite 41,'' repeated Thomas numbly. ''Wait a minute . . . my car . . .''

''Washed, waxed, and on its way back to your garage in Arlington.''

''Not so fast. You'll need the keys.'' He pulled out a leather-fobbed key set.

''We used a duplicate set.''

Somehow he wasn't surprised. ''I've got to get word to my financée.''

''She is being notified.''

''What are you telling her?''

''That you have a client emergency, and that you'll be away for a few days.''

''Hmph.'' They seemed to have figured all the angles. Or had they? ''There's a crew with a telescopic camera on a hill about a mile from your shop in Oldcolumbia.''

''We know. Routine industrial espionage.''

He gave up.

Wright pushed something into his hands. ''Here's your ticket, boarding pass, money. Goodbye, Mr. Thomas, we'll be in touch. Have a good trip!''

Holy moonrocks! Talk about being jerked around on a string! His thoughts were a total jumble. Penal Systems Inc. PSI. A cover . . . for what . . . for *whom*?

This crazy guillotine, he thought. Does Wright really know what he's talking about? I've got to get organized . . . after all, PSI is my client. I've got to start thinking like a lawyer. Suppose they actually use this damn thing on somebody? Execute some criminal, right there in the Lunaplex Rotunda. Would that constitute a public use that would start the year running for filing my c-i-p in the Federal Patent Office? Use wide open to the public view, he pondered, didn't necessarily make it anticipatory public use under the statute. We could claim it was just a test, he thought, an experiment to determine operability, as in the Elizabeth

Paving Block case. We—He inhaled suddenly with a sharp rasping sound.

This is insane.

I hope they take good care of my car.

His thoughts rambled on. An hour ago I was taking great pains to foul up their attempted physical. But looking back, apparently they liked what I did. I probably registered high on some sort of psi-lunacy index. Wright's call at the table . . . *that* wasn't from the lab. That was coming in from the moon! That was an okay from Lunaplex. Somebody out there liked me. Damn!

It's just too bloody mysterious. When I get back home . . . He studied his ticket as he walked up the ramp. It was one-way.

Strike that.

If I get back home . . .

3
Outward Bound

The tide is full, the moon lies fair.
   —Matthew Arnold, "Dover Beach"

Just as in his earlier lunar trip, the first thing that he noted within the narrow confines of his private compartment was—there was nothing special to be noted. There was no sense of the vastness of space, such as the early starmen had reported. In fact, someone had suggested that the whole thing was a hoax. You never saw the actual Earth falling away, or the actual moon looming up. All you ever saw was images on screens. And then you were finally underground, and moving down the stony corridors. You saw nothing; you might as well be back on Earth. (But how about that one-sixth gravity? There were some things that couldn't be faked.) Maybe it was all a comedy, but it was a very serious comedy.

He settled back in his recliner to catch the evening newscast. He was bored, and at first he heard the words but didn't catch the full impact.

". . . investigation of Michael Dore, the great philanthropist, the prime mover behind Lamplighters, the project that would ignite Jupiter, turn it into a small sun and make its moons habitable . . ." (Still that old hoax? thought Thomas. Doesn't anything else ever happen anywhere?) ". . . Dore admits that he has taken a lot of money, both from governments and from the private sector . . ." (Cut in with file tape of Dore's smiling face.) ". . . Mr. Dore not available for comment . . . rumored to be hiding on Luna. Predictions . . . Dore will be indicted for treason, embezzlement, and other assorted felonies, and he will be tracked down, arrested, tried in criminal court, and found guilty . . .''

Cut to mob chanting outside Lamplighter Headquarters in Washington, D.C.

> *Mikey Mikey ain't it fun!*
> *Stole the money, off he run!*
> *Sticky fingers, itchy feet*
> *Won't never give ole Jupe the heat!*

And then the chorus:

> *Mikey Mikey start the show!*
> *Light ole Jupe and make him go!*

Cut again to a churchyard somewhere on Maryland's Eastern Shore. A preacher stood on the front steps, haranguing a rapt audience. ''. . . this man is not one of us . . . 'Michael' means 'who is like God.' And it is written in the Book of Enoch that God gave Michael dominion over the sun, the stars, and all the lights in the sky. With what God has appointed, let not mortal hand interfere . . .''

Thomas frowned. He had the feeling that he was missing something very important. He bent forward.

Something nagged at him. There was more trivia. Somebody was explaining that Dore's anticipated arrest and trial had pushed aside matters of lesser moment. The Lunar Geologic Survey was delaying all seismic studies, pending outcome of the trial. Their little nuke buried near the Gagarin Crater hadn't even been connected. The big search for water would have to wait until after the treason trial of Michael Dore.

Treason? thought Thomas. Was that still punishable by death? Great bouncing basalts! He knew now why Lunar Judicial had ordered his guillotine.

He touched his throat in an uneasy gesture and turned off the holo. His armpits were damp.

He couldn't listen to any more of this. But the ship was still hours away from Lunaport. His eye caught something sticking up out of the side pocket. He pulled it out. A battered paperback, *Lunaplex on One Hundred Libras a Day*. He had to smile. How times had changed.

He read. He let his mind wander. He dozed. He awoke intermittently, and he thought of many things. How had he got into this mess? Was it the inevitable consequence of choosing the law as a career? Maybe the law was a mistake. His father (a Baptist minister) had reminded him of Martin Luther's admonition to *his* son: "Salvation is hard enough for theologians; a lawyer has no hope at all." He had often wondered what happened to Luther's son. One day he'd have to look it up. Anyhow, he, Quentin Thomas, had been firm in his choice of professions, and his father had actually helped him get a scholarship to Georgetown Law Seminary. "My son, promise me you'll not defend criminals." "I promise." "Get into corporation law," his father had suggested, "or family law, or admiralty, or tax, or even patents." So he had elected the patent courses. Intellectual Property, they called it at the seminary.

The first criminal he encountered was himself. He had ambivalent thoughts about that. No complaints, though; that was how he had met Nadys Blanding. All thought roads seemed to lead back to her.

He sighed, stuck the guidebook into an elastic pocket, stood up, stretched, and looked about him. Was he getting hungry? (That reminded him of *her*, again. Hunger was how they had met.) But he had better stop his daydreaming and give some thought to the present. But that, too, brought him back to Nadys. The day had started so simply. A nice visit with Nadys. (T—July 27?? He'd have to figure that out!) Then a pleasant lunch with Wright—pleasant up to a point, that is. Reviewing the cases, organizing the docket . . . and then—

Pow!

It had been that buffoonery in the PSI washroom, of course. He had intended it as simple retaliation to their deception. Had it annoyed them? Not a whit. They had been delighted. His display had but confirmed what they already strongly suspected—that he was a psi. And if they knew that much, they probably also knew that he had blind spots.

He wasn't a broad-spectrum psi. His sense of the future was limited, almost nil. He couldn't predict gyrations of the stock market, or the outcome of horse races. He was no good at the gambling casinos. He didn't know when the phone was about to ring, nor had he any premonitions when his parents died. Some psis could do all this, and more. Some could work with police to find killers. He couldn't. Some had known enough not to take passage on that doomed shuttle of '73. He couldn't do things like that. His psi, such as it was, lay almost entirely in the present. And it dealt with tiny things. He could "see" protons and neutrons and quarks and all the other minutiae that filled the shadow world between waves and solidity. He could follow electrons in their flight along conductors and circuitry. And he could do this over a fair distance: up to four or five kilometers, he estimated.

In his first week at the seminary he stood in front of the sandwich dispenser in Dolly's, off Wisconsin Avenue, and he could push the electrons along the proper circuits, and . . . click . . . and thlunk. And he would eat. He knew it wasn't right. He did it only because he was very hungry. His scholarship at the seminary was supposed to cover tuition and room and board, but somehow room and board got deleted in the computer logic circuitry. During his first week there he had slept on steam grates and park benches.

He had met Nadys late one night while he was sleeping on the hot-air vent outside the Law Library. She had taken him into her room for a couple of nights, until the landlady discovered him and threw him out. No matter; after that, things had suddenly improved. He liked to think about that remarkable afternoon in the bursar's office. He had just been sitting in the outer room, waiting to go in and complain again about the mixup, and he had let his mind run idly over their data bank circuitry. He had looked for his own entry, and he had found it easily. Oho, there was the glitch. The libras for room and board had indeed been punched in, but somehow had been almost immediately canceled. Somebody had touched the wrong key. Well, it was easily fixed. He adjusted the circuitry to show the original instructions, then prepared instructions for the check printer. Here, he remembered pausing a moment. In his course in Damages they were currently studying Punitive, and Pain and Suffering. PPS. Yes, we'll sprinkle a little PPS on our make-up check. Say five thousand libras. That brings it to five thousand two hundred and thirty. When the clerk called him, he was able to tell her, "I think that's my check over there in the printer."

He knew then that, if he could get close enough, he could break into any computer circuit, anywhere, any time. He fantasized about opening an account at Riggs, and then programming their data banks to send him a nice fat check periodically. But he didn't. And actually, as soon as he was out of seminary and working, he repaid the five thousand. But he had no regrets, either for the hunger, or for the healing theft.

He had considered making his talent available to the military or the intelligence agencies, but had thought better of it. He recognized intuitively that they wouldn't believe him; or, if they did, they would try to force him to do things he didn't want to do. In the end, they would kill him.

So he didn't advertise.

After he graduated from law seminary, one of his main objects in joining Laurence, Gottlieb had been simply to hide.

He had been on opposite sides with Nadys in their third year moot court case. After graduation, she had gone into the Patent Office, and he into private practice, and for a time they had lost touch.

He loved (and feared, and held in semi-contempt) the elegant ambiguities of the world of patents.

Mr. Gottlieb had undertaken to educate him in drafting a patent opinion for a valued client. "My boy," the senior partner had explained, "a report must be *true*. It has to be true as of the day you deliver it to the client. It has to be true five years later . . . even ten years later. And it has to maintain this truth despite fundamental changes in the fact pattern. It must be written so that it will be consistent with whatever develops."

"I don't understand."

"Look, let me show you something." Mr. Gottlieb had

given him a sheet of text. "That's page one of Delahunt's infringement report. We beat them in court last week. Look at *that*." He pointed to the summary.

"It says 'Your device infringes.'" Thomas was bewildered.

"Exactly. Clear, incisive . . . Wouldn't you agree?"

"Yes, sir."

"It's also unsophisticated, naive, and improvident. Because in a *second* opinion, they took it all back. *No* infringement, they said. They hadn't taken certain possible future changes in the fact pattern into account."

"And how is that done?"

"With weasel-words, my boy. Weasels. The necessities of life for the lawyer determined to survive."

"Weasels . . . ?"

"There are five basic weasels: double take, circular, laminated, labyrinthine, and dangling. You want examples?"

"That would help."

"Here's my list. Not exhaustive, of course."

The neophyte read:

1. Based on present information . . .
2. Based on the search results . . .
3. You have a substantial chance . . .
4. I stand with those who contend . . .
5. It appears that . . .
6. The risk appears to be no greater than average for this type of patent . . .
7. The patent risk appears to be within the business risk . . .
8. Within the parameters of this study . . .
9. Some courts would probably hold that . . .
10. Pursuant to your requirement to minimize expenses, we have restricted the scope of our study . . .

Good God, the new lawyer had thought. He had said, "I suppose you could combine some of these?"

"Oh, of course. In fact, the more the better. Say number

one plus number three plus number four, plus six, plus nine, and so on. That way we totally avoid the three major sins of the patent opinion.''

''Which are?''

''Clarity, completeness, and flat predictions.''

''I see.''

''Do you, now? I suppose you think that's the end of it?''

He knew it wasn't. But what else could there be?

''When you want to be really fuzzy,'' Mr. Gottlieb had said, ''you can refer to actual or hypothetical telephone conversations: 'We have amplified this point in previous informal conversations, and I am sure you understand the bearing on our conclusions.' ''

''But suppose he doesn't understand the bearing?''

''He'll never admit it,'' explained the other. ''It's the Emperor's New Clothes syndrome.''

That's the way it was at Laurence, Gottlieb. No one in the firm had ever suspected that he might be a psi, and he was quite happy to keep it that way. He just wanted to be a plain, ordinary human being and love Nadys. Oh, of course he had ambitions, but they all lay within his chosen professional sphere. He wanted to write the perfect patent specification, with the perfect patent claim, something so good it would be allowed on the first office action. He wanted to work with scientists and inventors—men and women at the scintillating edge of technology. That's all he really wanted.

How had he got into this rehash of history? He remembered now. He was hungry. He flipped the visiscreen for the menus. What was ship time? About twelve noon? Had they been en route a full day already? Evidently. So let's see. Call it brunch. He punched in for buttered biscuits, jam, and coffee. They popped out of the pneumo a few minutes later. As he sipped and munched, he thought again of Nadys. After graduation, he had next seen her on an examiner interview, on one of Penal Systems' applications in Group 220. She had been civil, even friendly, but that was as far as it went. She had helped him redraft his main apparatus claim, something about a seismic detector. He didn't try to make a date.

The next time was on an L.A. flight. He sat next to her. She was attending the International Patent Examiners Convention in Los Angeles. She was dressed differently. She *was* different. They shared the same table at the banquet. She seemed very like the Nadys of seminary days, when they were younger, and just a little foolish, and their future was an endless upward escalator. He had finished up with his client, then he had registered into her hotel. The convention broke up. They both stayed over.

For that remarkable weekend they had moved to a rundown but very private three-storey motel on the edge of the Great Barren, the (to some) beautiful escarpment left when LAX had slid into the sea in the quake of '36. Nadys had wanted to study the seismics, and he had wanted to study Nadys.

Her scent bewildered, enchanted, and finally enslaved him: some magic mixture of lilac and rose attar. It seemed to vary in intensity. Sometimes it was strong to the point of pungency. Other times it was so faint as to be almost undetectable. Always, though, it announced her presence like signals in his chip implants. It was nothing she touched to her skin from a bottle, nothing from a spray. Something she ate? He could never figure it out. Nor was it localized on any one part of her body. He had once stripped her down, and he had sniffed at her like a hound snuffling a trail along the ground. He had started with her perfumed black hair, and he had gone down her face, neck, underarms, breasts. Somewhere along the glamored undulance of her belly, olfactory paralysis set in and he had had to abandon his investigation. He had ceased temporarily to be able to smell anything, sense anything. He was like a wine taster who had sampled until his palate was dead.

Stranger still, he was the only one who could smell her. No one else was aware of it, not even she. Indeed, she refused to believe she had it. Sometimes he thought it must be some bizarre scentless molecule that his nasal mucosa took from her and which his own unique body chemistry converted to the actual perfume. Rather like a chemical equivalent of fluorescence, where an atom takes in a photon at an invisible frequency and releases another at a visible frequency.

He had interviewed her on another Penal Systems application a week after their return from L.A. This time, to his consternation and chagrin, she was cold and uncooperative. (What the hell! he thought. What's going on?) He demanded that they see her primary, and they went in together. The primary agreed with her, and actually seemed almost embarrassed. "What you have here is really a rather inept claim, Mr. Thomas. The case does appear to present patentable subject matter, but you have to claim it in a way that distinguishes from the prior art, but at the same time recites all the essential elements of the invention. And remember, the claim is the direct object of the two-word sentence, 'I claim,' or "We claim.' It isn't a summary, such as one might read in Chem Abstracts." The primary had looked over at Nadys, frowning slightly. "Perhaps Miss Blanding can help you draft something more to the point."

"Yes," she clipped.

He followed her out, not quite sure whether he had any right to be angry, and he had to hurry to keep up.

She scribbled out something as soon as they sat down again in her office. "New damn main claim. Here's a damn copy for you. Four and five are dependent."

He looked at it, and it was perfect. It was awesome. How did she do it? His anger (not really very much) evaporated. He said, "Will you marry me? Seriously, I mean?"

"Will you ever learn to write a simple apparatus claim?"

"I'm at the Marriott."

"Room 1302."

(Well, I'll be darned.) He folded up his case file and walked out.

He had left his door ajar, and he had barely got inside when she opened it without knocking. He walked back and closed the door as she stripped. He noted, marveling, that she wore neither panties nor brassiere. She had planned it this way all along.

The scent of unnamed flowers was overwhelming.

She said softly, "Let us dance."

Some weeks later, as he watched her glide in nude grace over the deep pile of his bedroom carpet, with her black-gold hair resonant on her white shoulders, he growled, "One million gold dinars for that female."

"What *are* you talking about?"

"I'm glad you asked." He told her about a chapter in Sir Hillary Benton's *Byzantine Byways*. "Süleyman the Magnificent," he explained, "drew an outline of a woman's body on a piece of plywood. The court carpenter cut it out so as to present the figure full-face. That is, he left the aperture."

"Plywood? In the sixteenth century?"

"Well, whatever they used then. Do you want to hear this, or not?"

"Go ahead. A vacancy in the seraglio, I presume."

"In those days, woman, it was an honor. A strictly invitational situation. Well, anyway, he gave the cutout to the deputy vizier and told him to scour the kingdom for a woman who would fit exactly into the aperture. Well, they hunted for years. They kept raising the price. You'd be surprised if you knew some of the things those poor women did, or had done to them, so they would fit in the cut out."

"The original liposuction?"

"A lot bloodier. You want to hear this, or not?"

"You keep saying that. Get to the point."

"Come over here. It's classified. I have to whisper."

She lay down beside him, very suspicious, but very curious. He ran his hands along the sides of her body, and then to her breasts. Her nipples rose, red and hard. "I have seen the template," he said with quiet authority. "It's in the Mellon Museum of Islamic Art, in D.C. And you, my dear Nadys, have the exact same configuration. You would fit precisely. In 1530 I could have sold you to the deputy vizier for one million gold dinars, tax free."

"Would you have?"

"Certainly not."

"I don't believe you."

"I—"

"Did Süleyman ever find his ideal female?"

"Well, yes, he did. A rather odd coincidence, according to Sir Hillary. She was a slave girl, working in the castle kitchen. She had been there all the time."

"So look at all the money he saved."

"Not only that. Every day at noon, just before muezzin, she brought him beer and pizza. And there were other similarities."

"Similarities?"

"To you, I mean."

"Like maybe her name was Nadys?"

"How did you guess? And I'm sure you know what 'Nadys' means in Arabic?"

"Tell me. What does 'Nadys' mean in Arabic?"

"It means, sweetheart, 'she who brings beer and pizza.' So, would you, please? On the dresser . . . I think there are still a couple of slices. Hey, love?"

She hesitated only milliseconds. Then, in a blurred leap, she was at the dresser and then back to the bed. She ripped the sheet back. She rubbed the pizza in his protesting unprotected face. She doused him with cold beer. All this in silence.

He grabbed her down, pinned her under him. She bit him on the face, lips, shoulders. The teeth bruises would stay with him for days.

After it was over, with her arms and legs still locked around him, she told him what she thought of him. He could only groan in gratified agreement. Yes, there was no Sir Hillary, no template, no million gold dinars, no slave girl. You (he licked tomato sauce and mozzarella cheese from her right breast), my priceless darling, are the only reality. And there's no way I can explain you to Mr. Gottlieb. So why don't we take a shower together and inspect each other for anchovies and stray pepperoni slices?

Oh, Nadys, Nadys. What indeed is the meaning of Nadys? What alien tongue gives birth to so strange a word? A word-at-large. Give it your own meaning. Gorgeous. Passionate. Brilliant. (Like one of Poe's erudite fictional females?)

4
Rock 10017

Go visit it by the pale moonlight.
   —*Sir Walter Scott, "The Lay of the Last Minstrel"*

After the shuttle docked, Quentin Thomas exited down the ramp toward customs.

He had immediate problems with the one-sixth gravity, and he realized that he had forgotten to take his Baryx pills. They were supposed to make you feel heavy. He doubted that. Actually, though, a proper dose seemed to give your legs better coordination. No matter. In an hour or so he'd be pretty well adjusted.

Behind him he noted the landing crew bringing up lines to drain the shuttle water tanks. All incoming ships had to bring in a certain amount of water, generally proportional to ship weight, or pay an exhorbitant fine. Water was life, but it seemed to vanish as soon as it arrived. You drank it, then exhaled and excreted it, and some was captured and processed and recycled, but there was always a net deficit. The very walls seemed to soak it up. All surfaces were carefully waterproofed with acrylics, but the efforts merely slowed the absorption. You exhaled, the walls inhaled.

Our bodies, he mused, are simply a conduit for this remarkable oxide of hydrogen. We are temporary reservoirs. In, out. We are hardly aware of water—until we are deprived of it. All the works of man float on water. We grow our crops with it. Our ships sail upon it. We fish in it. Our factories guzzle it. Lunaplex cries for it.

Water, so simple, so complex. Not just H_2O. More like a liquid crystal. The molecules form stringy clusters of pseudocrystals like SiO_2 in quartz, rather like wood fibers. He had read somewhere that, with an assured one hundred liters per minute of fresh water, Lunaplex could open that long-awaited hospital for cardiacs and semiparalytics, and perhaps have enough left over for a little light industry. Trivial things, true; nothing like Dore's grandiose fantasies. Yet real, and trembling on the edge of the possible.

Well, enough of futile mental meanderings about water. Not his concern. He wouldn't be here long enough to be affected by it one way or the other.

Should he try to call Nadys? No. Back in Maryland it was the middle of the night. Not too many meters overhead, sunlight was being converted into moonlight, and that moonlight would, sometime tonight, shine into Nadys's bedroom window at Patuxent Haven. He smiled. It's a small solar system.

Customs was jammed. There were four lines of passengers awaiting clearance. He sighed and got in one of the lines.

He noticed that armed guards stood at the gates that led to the buses. Odd. There has been nothing like this on his first trip. But he figured it out quickly. Most of these people were here because they smelled blood, in the form of the approaching trial of Michael Dore. They were reporters, writers, idle court-followers. They would have held ringside boxes at Nero's circuses. The police were here as a presence, to preserve order.

His head jerked. "Mr. Quentin Thomas!" They were calling him on the speaker system. "Mr. Quentin Thomas, report to Room 5. Mr. Thomas, Room 5."

What's up? he thought. And where is Room 5? He ran his eyes around the edge of the customs chamber. There it was. He left the line, worked his way over. A guard barred him at the door. "I'm Thomas," he explained. The guard opened the door for him.

The man at the desk looked up. "Thomas?"

"Yes."

"You have a bill of lading?"

The lawyer handed over the manifest Wright had given him. The agent looked at it, then handed it back.

"Everything's in order, Mr. Thomas. They're loading your crate on a van. You're expected to ride with cargo to the Rotunda. All charges have been paid. A crew will meet you there."

"That's fine. Thank you."

The douanier grunted and motioned to the exit behind him.

Thomas rode up front with the driver, a taciturn man of negligible curiosity and zero communication skills. Which was just as well. The lawyer didn't want to talk.

Already his nose was itching: the standard response to the lunar dryness and the smell of lunar rock, never really completely sealed off by layers of plastic. The net effect was something oddly sulfurous, yet clean, sterile, as in a hospital.

The route actually seemed to encourage silence. The road was a ten-kilometer underground freight and passenger highway, well-lit, straight, monotonous.

On his earlier trip the limo driver had stopped in mid-tunnel and had invited his passengers to "be quiet, and listen." And in the gathering silence they had listened in wonder to barely audible sublunar crunches, whispers, groans. Far below, the lunar interior was alive. Revolving Mother Earth created tidal stresses in her daughter that sounded like leviathans battling in a distant deep.

He wet his lips. He'd have to remember to get ointment for chapped lips. No, forget it. He wouldn't be here that long.

The last time he had been here he had loved it: the things to see, the one-sixth gravity . . . everything was exhilarating. But now . . . all he could think of was, get this thing set up, see the stranger in 41, cancel his own room reservation, then get out. He intended to be on the next shuttle home.

Lunaplex was diminutive, yet thoroughly multinational. The Russians had contributed their great Bolshoi Ballet, the Austrians their Lippizaner Horse Show (with leaps thirty feet high), the English the local legal system (hail, lord chancellor), the Americans their Armstrong-Aldrin Inn and a pizza parlor that rivaled anything in Manhattan. And so it went.

The minimetropolis was too small, too young, too underpopulated to have a true culture. For that they would need a few bona fide heroes, some noteworthy villains, and a mix of solid citizens in between. Perhaps that would come. All too soon, perhaps. Meanwhile, what they did have was entertainment. On his prior visit he had wandered around the Plex all night. He'd seen the marvelous show at the ballet, he'd watched the acrobats at the circus, somewhere in a corridor off the Rotunda. He had had a couple of drinks at the Bar-Del-O (where he had made light conversation with various ladies and had turned down some interesting invitations). His sundry circadian rhythms had got totally out of synch, and he hadn't minded at all.

Not this time.

Now, all he could think about was getting this project finished and returning to Nadys. He wondered if she missed him as much as he missed her. Probably not. Women are different. They can be pretty emotional at times, and they can be mysterious and difficult to fathom. Well, maybe she missed him a little.

The van drove right into the central grid and into the Rotunda, where three men were waiting. One of them stepped forward. "You Mr. Thomas?"

The lawyer stuck his head out the window. "I'm Thomas. You the bailiff?"

"Yes, sir. We're supposed to help you set it up." He called to the driver, "Hey, mac, can you back it up over here? To the middle, in front of the rock?"

The silent man nodded as he maneuvered the vehicle toward what appeared to be a big black rock sunk in the center of the Rotunda. And finally he talked. He asked Thomas, "What you got here, buddy?"

The lawyer answered as he got out of the van. "Guillotine." He looked up, far overhead into the majestic vault of the dome.

"You mean, like for killing people?"

"We prefer to call it 'execution.'"

"God help me." It was a solemn whisper.

Not an uncommon expression around a guillotine, thought

the lawyer. He watched the driver gun the motor, then the van screeched away.

The bailiff and his men were ready with their tools. Thomas explained how to position the crate. They worked silently, save for a few grunts and subdued curses. They moved easily, obviously long accustomed to the low gravity. The scaffolding went up, then the neck rest, the blade was inserted in the runners, and finally the motor was connected.

Halfway into the job a couple of very bored camera crews rolled up, set up their lights and equipment, took a few shots, then decided to hold off awhile.

This would probably be on the news, thought Thomas. Nadys would see it. At least she would know where he was. She would also wonder why he hadn't told her. Told her what? That he had been shanghaied?

The assembly was completed in half an hour. Now he'd have to test it. He ran the blade up. The holo crews came to life once more. In a conventional guillotine the blade would drop automatically as soon as it reached the top of the scaffolding. This one, though, had to get a signal from one of three button-terminated cables. The computer in the base would select one at random. He handed the cables to the three workmen. "When I say 'Hit,' press your button." He waited a moment. The cameras were taking it all in. "Hit!"

The blade flashed down. Clunk.

He was beginning to feel queasy.

He collected the cables, locked them in the control box, double-locked the blade, and gave the key to the crew leader.

"Is that all?" said the bailiff. "Isn't there another key? To this panel?" He pointed.

The lawyer shrugged. "This panel has a five-letter code key, and they didn't give it to me." He had already traced along some intricate circuitry connected to the randomizer in the machine's computer. That circuitry had a life, a *raison d'être* all its own. It very effectively locked the panel, behind which lay an electronic entity even more mysterious, a thing that had nothing to do with the guillotine. He hadn't the faintest idea what it was. Why hadn't Wright mentioned this? How could PSI expect competent patent coverage on their crazy infernal machine when they continually kept him in the dark? Didn't they trust him? The omission went beyond mere frustration—it verged on humiliation. *Who* was doing *what* to him? And behind his back? He fought down a rising anger. All right, he concluded. For now, let it be. It's their problem. But he had to say something plausible to this officer of the court.

He temporized. "Looks like this opens to the motor drive and batteries. If the drive fails, you may have to break the lock."

The crew leader looked dubious; then he shrugged. "Leave it go. Wait till we have a problem." He turned and motioned his two assistants to follow him out. The cameramen had already packed up and left.

Something fluttered past the lawyer's face, and he ducked by reflex. The thing slithered and jerked in a weird skittering flight path. A slithy tove, mused Thomas, gyring and gimbling in the wabe. In the midst of death, life waltzes on. A moth? Insects here? Well, why not? And do they undergo special evolution in response to the one-sixth gravity, and fill predestined niches, like the finches in Darwin's Galápagos studies? How do they get here? With the flora, probably. The biggest moth on Terra is already the luna moth. What would *they* evolve into here? And would their predator bats evolve proportionately? Fortunately, not his problem.

Quentin Thomas was alone. He let himself sink slowly into the near silence. It reminded him of the opening lines in Gray's "Elegy."

> *The curfew tolls the knell of parting day,*
> *The lowing herd wind slowly o'er the lea,*
> *The plowman homeward plods his weary way,*
> *And leaves the world to darkness and to me.*

Interesting rhythm. Iambic pentameter? Would it work with the guillotine? The main claim might begin:
A *blade* af*fixed* be*tween* two *guides* . . .
Only tetrameter. Try again.
. . . be*tween* two *up*right *guides* . . .

Pentameter, but still not quite right. He wished Nadys were here. She could fix it.

They had danced nude that time at the Marriott. His mind and body, reticulated, interwoven with hers, living, pulsing. She had taught him (rather, *tried* to teach him) the rhythms of claim writing. ''You have to release your cerebral neurotransmitters . . . the same way as a musician. A good claim can be like a waltz: three-quarter time is excellent. Strauss. *The Blue Danube. Tales from the Vienna Woods. The Emperor Waltz*. That's all dactyl—*one* two three, *dah* di di. '*List*en my *chil*dren and *you* shall *hear*.' Not perfect dactyl, but you get the idea. 'I *sprang* to the *stir*rup and *Jor*is and *he* . . . ' That's a little better, isn't it? Anapest is quite similar: two di's and then the dah. 'You are *old* Father *Will*iam the *young* man *said*.' '*Pro*cess com*pris*ing re*act*ing a *res*in . . . ' Music! You should definitely hear music! '*Meth*od of *form*ing a *wat*erproofed *coat*ing . . . ' Got it? '*Play* us a *tune* on an *un*broken *spin*et.' You hear? '*This* is the *for*est pri*me*val/the *mur*muring *pines* and the *hem*locks . . . ' '*Pro*duct con*tain*ing in *parts* by *weight*/for*ty* of iso*cy*anate . . . ' Perhaps you should listen to some classical music when you draft your claims. I'll give you some tapes.''

He recalled how the weird fad of claim rhythm had originated. *Ex parte Radix*, the famous patent case, had gone to the Supreme Court, and the Chief Justice had refused to vote. The C.J. (a Ph.D. in Elizabethan literature, with youthful pieces in *North American Poetry*, and an accomplished amateur cellist) abstained with a brief but blistering comment: ''Claim One is nonsense, but it is not *mere* nonsense. It is raucous, cacaphonous nonsense. At least Edward Lear blessed *his* nonsense with rhyme and rhythm. I cannot understand how the commissioner permitted this profanation of our Mother Tongue to exit the Patent Office.''

Now, of course *all* patent cases going to the Supreme Court were traumatic events for the Patent Office and the patent bar. This was always especially true for the hapless commissioner, who had the task of explaining the new decision to staff and public, and of establishing new practice guidelines conforming to the new case. This was not easily done. The Court's attempts to clarify a knotty point in patent law had once been compared to efforts of a hammer-wielding chimpanzee to repair a mainframe computer. In short, the Supreme Court gave the Patent Office the heebie-jeebies. The other high court patent cases were bad enough. But *Radix* was special: the commissioner had been mentioned personally. And (as in a semicondutor), his response far exceeded the stimulus. It was rumored that he took two wrong turns in driving home from Crystal Plaza that fateful decision day, and that when he finally opened his front door, he could not remember the names of his wife and children. No matter. By the time he entered his seventh floor suite the next morning, he had formulated a Plan. He knew (or thought he knew) exactly what the C.J. wanted. Working through a staff of dedicated deputies, he set up seminars with experts in literature, language, and poetry. Especially poetry. The group supervisors and primaries dutifully attended these seminars. They learned rhyme. They learned rhythm. And the Word slowly filtered down into the ranks of examiners and assistant examiners. Notices appeared in the Official Gazette explaining the new guidelines. Rhyme and rhythm were henceforth required, with retention of sense and coherence where possible. But just then the country elected a new president, who appointed a new commissioner. *He* left enforcement of the R and R rules to the discretion of the individual examining groups. Some used it, some didn't. Nadys's group stayed with it.

He remembered.

Ah yes, that evening, in his room at the Marriott, they had danced nude.

Oh Nadys, Nadys.

"What are you thinking?" she had whispered.

What had he been thinking? He had been thinking of Dostoyevski and how the great Russian writer, in making love with his beloved Anna Grigorievna, started by kissing her body, beginning with her face, her lips, then her breasts, and working down, down . . . biting her a little, here and there.

He whispered back: "All this is going on tape, you know. I'm sending copies to your super and to the commissioner as firm evidence of cooperation between examiner and attorney. The commissioner's going to use it as part of his induction program for new examiners. Now, sweetheart, if you could just make a quarter turn toward the camera, we can get a profile of your, ah, lovely, ah, dactyls. *Ow!*'' He still bore the scar over his right nipple. Two stitches and a tetanus booster had been required. She cried when she saw what she had done, but she never apologized. No doubt about it. She loved him.

And so back to a harsher reality.

He left the death-engine and walked over to the center of the Rotunda. Ah, yes, the thing he looked for was still there. Once a wonder, now a reproach.

Rising from the floor was a dark irregular shape—a basalt rock. Bolted to the side of the rock was a golden plaque. The lawyer read it with mixed feelings, including a strong sense of desecration.

Rock 10017

This rock was formed from molten lava 3.6 billion years ago. About 500 million years ago, a meteorite shattered the bedrock and thrust the rock up into the lunar soil, just under the surface. Six million years ago another impact tossed the rock out onto the surface, where in July 1969 the men of Apollo 11 found it and brought it to Earth. During the Lunar Centennial it was returned here.

He sighed and looked up into the dome. On Earth, at new moon, with good binoculars, you could pick out this dome as a sturdy light-point: the only illumination on our little sister planet. Blazoned across the inner crest of the great structure in luminous alabaster letters was an inscription:

FIAT IVSTITIA ET RVANT COELI

which, he supposed, translated as, 'Let justice be done though the heavens fall.' Hopefully such drastic measures would never be required!

Except for this dome, all Lunaplex lay under a ten-meter-thick layer of lunar aggregate, protection against extremes of cold and sun-heat, and against all but the biggest meteors.

The dome, however, crested through that ten-meter layer out into the lunar landscape, like an expression of architectural defiance determined to dominate a jumble of aeons-old lesser silicate monuments.

He looked up again. Suppose a wandering meteorite knocked the dome in? Wouldn't all the air in Lunaplex rush out through the wound, like blood through a severed jugular? No. He knew the answer to that. There were seal doors all over the place. They responded automatically to pressure drops. The Rotunda would be sealed off all around, within minutes of the break-in. Also, the great iris at the bottom of the dome would fan out, and air loss would come to a whistling stop.

He walked on.

Slightly off-center within the circle of the Rotunda stood the French Fountain. But, of course, without water. A pumping system and a great empty tank awaited somewhere underground. One day (maybe) the tank would be full of water and the pumps would be hurling it up high overhead, six times higher than terrestrial gravity had permitted. Ah, what a sight that would be! But he doubted that it would happen in his lifetime. Too bad, he thought, recalling the story. This exquisite baroque bronze work had been presented on permanent loan by the Tenth Republic of France, as though to give a Gallic touch to distant Lunaplex. It had been designed by Madame de Maintenon for a jaded Louis XIV, and it had been intended for an intimate nook of the Grand Trianon at Versailles. The three spigots (*les trois jettes*) were supposed to arc their lacy streams into high, nicely calculated parabolas, to meet in frothy overhead exuberance, fall into the higher basin, which then overflowed to the walled pool. The immortal Maintenon had even named the three spigots, and you could read the names (in Latin, of course) in bronze bas-relief: *Purgaro* ("I purify"), *Capero* ("I charm"), and *Recrearo* ("I refresh"). He walked over, sat on the pool edge, and looked up. He could imagine the eager streams rushing high, joining, crashing down; the upper basin spilling over and over and over; and a circular curtain careening down. And then down the drains, and recycle, and up again. Even without water it could hypnotize you. That Maintenon was one smart biddy. He wondered if Louis had ever sat here (maybe on a satin cushion), and had he taken off his high-heel shoes and his white silk stockings and dangled the royal tootsies in this early Jacuzzi?

He bent over to pick up a battered beer can inside the empty pool and looked around for a trash receptacle. Yes, over there.

The Rotunda opened on four wings. The first was the Commercial Alcove, where practically all lunar business was handled: the Geologic Survey, Exploration, Transport, Construction, Finance, and the Cafeteria. He remembered some of this from his prior trip, and some from the paperback on the incoming shuttle.

Just inside the corridor leading to Wing Number 1 was an exhibit case containing a pumpkin-size replica of Luna, with an explanation card at the side. It was a model demonstrating the planned nuke shot (Project Hydro) on the other side of the moon. It would be the starting gun for the great seismic search for water. The vibrations would go around and through the moon core and would be picked up by seismic equipment spaced at intervals around the lunar surface. Wave patterns would be analyzed for deposits of hydrated minerals. There were sample squiggles on recording paper with arrows pointing to allophane, apophyllite . . . all the way down to zoisite. Nothing for H_2O per se, of course. Nobody was that optimistic.

Thomas thought about the upcoming exploration. With the nuke shot as epicenter, the artificial moonquake would come to its nodal focus . . . where? Right here under Lunaplex? He hoped the Geological Survey knew what they were doing. Then he shrugged and shook his head. None of his business. He'd be long gone before the shot, anyhow.

In the second wing were Land Records, Vital Statistics (Weddings, Births, Deaths); Libraries (General, Technical, Legal).

In Wing 3 were Law Enforcement, Police, and Detention.

The Fourth Wing was the Courtroom. When he had been here before it had still been under construction. He walked over, peeked through the thick glass door panel into the darkened room, and felt strangely uneasy. What was wrong

with him? It was a perfectly normal courtroom. The interior
was lined with highly polished dark green lunar olivine
columns, alternating with wide ebony panels. The floor,
like the Rotunda border, was alternating black and white
parquet. He seemed to recall that the black squares were
local ilmenite, the white ones were anorthosite.

At the rear was the lord chancellor's raised dais, on a
level with the witness chair. Thick tapestries were hung
behind the dais. In front, to the chancellor's left, was a jury
box. Counsel tables equipped with computer terminals faced
the bench. Overhead, in the mezzanine, were enclosures for
the media: the press, holo crews, visiting officials.

Finally, in the entranceway, the catch-as-catch-can audience benches for ordinary citizenry. All these spaces
would soon be packed. But not for him. As soon as he had
talked to his mysterious contact in 41 he was headed for
the next flight back to Terra. The nooner-lunar. It would
be easy to get a reservation. Everybody was coming in—
for the expected trial of Michael Dore, he supposed. He
had heard on the ship yesterday that scalpers were getting
ten thousand libras for a sit-up ticket on incoming over-
crowded ramshackled commuters. But there was all sorts
of cheap space returning.

This courtroom (so he had read) was a study in extremes.
This, the newest hall of justice in the terrestrial/lunar ju-
diciary, contained some of the oldest oddments. The witness
chair was assembled from pieces of wood rescued from
chairs famous in criminal history. It included, for example,
something from the chair in which, in the year 1440, the
infamous Gilles de Rais had sat (or, it was plausibly rumored, refused to sit) when condemned by an indignant
French peerage for the torture-murders of over one hundred
peasant boys. This composite chair also included an arm of
the chair in which Mrs. Surratt (innocent and doomed) had
been questioned following Lincoln's assassination. Also included were wooden souvenirs of the Stamford Strangler,
the Richmond (Indiana) Ripper, and a piece of the chair
once warmed by Eichmann of Holocaust fame. Plus an
ebony cross-leg from the chair in which Galileo had so

prudently changed his mind during his examination by the Italian Inquisition.

This thing, this piece of horror furniture (so Thomas had read) had been assembled by the lord chancellor himself, the Honorable Martin Rile. ''Brings out the truth in a man,'' his lordship had explained. ''In my court you don't need a truth drug.''

As in British criminal courtrooms, a trapdoor and stairs behind the chair led down to a holding area, where the defendant and perhaps certain witnesses were held until called up.

Michael Dore would so arise, as from up out of hell, to meet an earthly doom. Make that lunar doom, reflected Thomas. He shivered. It must be cooling off in the Rotunda.

If found guilty, the archcriminal would be taken (walked? carried? dragged?) through that central courtroom aisle and out through these doors. Thomas turned and looked behind him.

Dore would be taken over there, to the machine. The blade would be raised in metallic majesty. Dore's body would be stretched out on his chest, his neck fitted into the notch.

The lawyer's stomach was writhing. He ran over to a bed of tulips, and there he vomited. After a time he faced back to the Death waiting by the rock. ''Forgive me,'' he whispered. For what? He wasn't sure. Nor was he too clear as to whom he addressed the petition. God? NASA? No. More likely he begged pardon of the great simple men of Apollo 11: Armstrong, Aldrin, Collins . . .

His eyes returned to the great blade, now somber, silent, but pulsing murder even as it rested.

One giant step for mankind.

He looked at his watch. It was time to contact the mystery man (or woman?) in the A-A Inn. Then he could leave this place that he had made terrible.

He walked over to the line of autocarts, climbed into the first one, and tried to remember how to operate it. Yes, there's the coin slot. A copper thaler would take you anywhere in the Plex. And now the map light comes on, with buttons to punch for your destination. Everything radiated outward from the Rotunda, like spokes on a wheel. He punched "A-A" and listened with ear and mind as the circuitry moved into action. Yes, it seemed to be working perfectly. The circuit chip should order the steering mechanism to bring the cart counter-clockwise into the outer circle of the Rotunda, then take the first fork to the right. He followed the electron flow, anticipating the mindless obedience of the machinery at each step. Ingenious little creatures. Probably patented? Actually, this one cart might have produced a bundle of patents. He found himself thinking about how he would organize the patent program, what cases would have to be filed, and the structure of some of the main claims. Hey, stop this! This isn't a busman's holiday. Just check in with this person at A-A, then get out. OUT.

And so here we are, right up into the check-in area of the Armstrong-Aldrin Inn. He read the elapsed time on the LED: four minutes. He could have walked.

He checked in at the desk to make sure his bag had arrived and was told it had been placed in his room. He started to explain to the clerk that he wasn't staying over, then decided it would be futile. He got directions for Room 41.

5
Attorney and Client

Ill met by moonlight.
   —*William Shakespeare, A Midsummer Night's Dream*

As he approached the door to Number 41, Thomas heard a strange sound—a *rumbling*? Then he caught it: a drum roll. And not just any drum roll. He frowned. It was the *chamade*, played by the drummer who accompanied the guillotine. It was the last sound heard by the criminal. A final percussive reminder of a life gone awry.

He gulped and almost stumbled. This was coming from 41.

The person (male? female?) he was to see was demonstrating incredibly bad taste.

He clenched his jaw and pressed the announce button.

"Enter," commanded the phono. It was a strong but well-modulated male voice.

Thomas twisted the doorknob. It would not turn. Does the occupant know the door is locked? he wondered. It seemed likely. So now what? Was this another test? He sighed. This was becoming irksome. He examined the latch work. There were actually two locks, above and below the knob. Each had a grid of twenty-five letter-buttons. The two locks had to be activated simultaneously, or neither worked. Not easy for the combination holder to get in, much less an outsider. Well, get to it. He sent exploratory feelers inside the upper, then the lower. The upper had a four-letter solution. He worked on it while he checked the lower lock. More complicated. Seven letters. Working . . . working . . . Now he had them both. Upper: JOVE . . . No, make that

46

IOVE. Lower: ARDEBIT. IOVE ARDEBIT. More Latin. Was that supposed to mean something? He could make a wild guess. "Jupiter will burn." The rally cry of the Lamplighters. How could anyone be so credulous?

"Enter," the man had said. So he would enter. With his index finger he punched in the "hold" button, then the letters, then "release." Click. The door opened almost instantly. Someone was standing there in the hallway waiting for him.

Thomas looked up at a pleasant gray-haired man, perhaps in his late fifties, half a head taller than himself. He stared, blinking, unbelieving. He stammered, "But you're . . ."

"Dore. It's a pleasure, Mr. Thomas, please come in." He held out his hand, which Thomas shook almost unwittingly.

"But—" began the lawyer.

Dore closed the door behind him, then held up a forefinger: the universal signal for "We are bugged." He pointed to his left ear. Thomas sensed a faint buzzing. He willed his cranial receptors to tune in. The buzzing faded. Dore's mental signals were coming in clearly.

"I asked Wright not to tell you whom you were to meet," signaled the tall man. "We didn't want to shock you. It just seemed best, particularly in case they gave you a bad time at customs."

"No problems there. They knew I was bringing in the—" He paused and gulped.

Dore smiled. "The guillotine, Mr. Thomas?"

"Yes, sir."

"Call me Mike."

"Yes, sir. Mike."

"The guillotine was your cover. I don't think we could have gotten you here without it."

"Oh?" *Cover?* He looked around uneasily. What was he mixed up in?

Dore laughed. "You heard the drum rolls?"

Thomas nodded.

"Just my keyboard." He indicated a flat piano keyboard on the side table. "I amuse myself. Actually, I prefer

Bach and Beethoven to the chamade. But you still need drums. Ludwig's great violin concerto starts with a drumbeat, you'll recall. Later on perhaps I can give you a recital.''

Thomas shielded certain thoughts concerning the other's mental stability. Then he signaled: ''I was told to contact you.''

''Yes. Of course. Let's sit down, Quentin, and I'll try to explain why you're here.''

Thomas again shielded certain thoughts equivalent to, ''It's about time.'' He sat down.

Dore pushed a button. Wineglasses and a bottle moved out onto a side shelf. ''A little wine?''

Thomas shook his head. It had been a long day, and he knew it would hit him like a sledgehammer.

Dore sat down again. He signaled, ''What do you know about the Lamplighters?''

The lawyer didn't know how to answer that. ''I have no special knowledge. Just what I see on the holos and read in the papers. According to them, Jupiter was supposed to turn into a small sun, warm up its moons, and then our excess population could be shipped out there.''

''That's it, essentially. The ignition will begin when enough nuclear waste material is dumped into the Great Red Spot—the GRS. Jupiter is mostly hydrogen. This hydrogen will begin to fuse into helium, with release of tremendous amounts of energy. The planet will glow red, and it will expand. First off, it will eat the four tiny inner moons, 1979 J3, Adrastea, Amalthea, and 1979 J2.''

''What about Io?'' asked Thomas. ''Don't they have an observatory or something on Io?''

''Yes, we have a station there, the Arthur Clarke. It will have to be evacuated. Io will be melted down and absorbed into the new sun.''

''What happens to the outer moons?''

''The other three Galileans—Europa, Ganymede, and Callisto—will be in good shape. They'll have temperate climates. Their ice sheets will melt into lakes and oceans. The residual land should be reasonably arable, and the total new land should be about forty percent that of Earth. That's more than Columbus added in 1492. The population prospects are fantastic.''

Dore began striding back and forth across the room. His voice signals seemed to glow. ''Think of it, Quentin! The Lamplighters will bring in a new civilization. Long ago we disposed of nuclear waste by shooting it into the sun. It was clean, easy, simple. Then, about ten years ago, along came the Lamplighters: 'You're wasting all this waste,' we said. 'Send it to Jupiter.' '' He stopped in mid-stride and looked down at Thomas. ''The astro boys say Jupiter is a failed sun. If it had picked up a little more mass when the planets were forming five billion years ago, it would have turned on. We'd have a two-sun system. That was the dream of the great imagineer, Arthur Clarke. Great idea, said the astrophysicists. But when you really analyzed it, you found Jupiter would need fifty times its present mass to give the temperatures and pressures necessary to start a nuclear reaction. No, said the scientists, Jupiter doesn't have the mass, and it will never have the mass. So? Enter us, the Lamplighters. 'Mass?' we said. 'Who needs mass? Radioactivity will do it. Just a few million tons of nuclear waste.' '' He grinned. ''So Jupiter is now the biggest garbage dump in the solar system.'' He resumed striding, as though punctuating his mental transmissions pedometrically. ''We send all our killer garbage to Station Arthur Clarke on Io. The crew there repacks it and shoots it into the GRS. Jupiter is full of hydrogen. At the appointed hour radioactivity will ignite that hydrogen and Jupiter will become a small red sun.''

Thomas shielded his thoughts. The appointed hour? That's the problem, isn't it? The hour is upon us, and no ignition in sight.

Dore paused, lost in his own thoughts. In an absent gesture he picked up his keyboard and ran a scale. Thomas said nothing. He watched the delicate wineglasses dance. Careful, he thought, another half octave and they'll shatter.

Dore laid the instrument aside gently. When he signaled again, it seemed to Thomas to be more like an introspective monologue. ''I've given the last ten years to the project.

I got the basic idea from the early science-fiction novels of Arthur Clarke, of course, where he had a titanic intellect turn Jupiter into a second sun. Actually, you know, I'm not the first to try. Lamplighters had a couple of predecessors, but they failed, rather like De Lesseps failing at Panama. One of the earlier groups built the station on Io—really a big mistake. Far too close, when Jupiter ignites. Well, I've spent most of my considerable personal fortune. And now the whole thing is about to come crashing down about my ears. I have powerful enemies, Quentin, people who want the project to fail. People who will be badly hurt if it succeeds." He looked thoughtfully at his young visitor. "I was indicted yesterday, while you were en route here."

Thomas nodded. So it had come.

"The charge," continued Dore, "is treason. You know that if I am found guilty, I can be executed?"

"You can appeal," said Thomas nervously.

"No. There's no appeal. Under the Lunar Statutes the trial before the lord chancellor is conclusive."

Thomas felt a growing sense of horror. They hadn't mentioned this at Georgetown.

"So I'll need a good lawyer," said Dore.

Thomas very suddenly understood a great deal. "Good heavens, Mike! No! *Not me!*"

His host simply smiled genially at him.

Thomas signaled urgently: "Am I getting through to you?"

Dore held up a circled thumb and forefinger—the universal "yes."

The lawyer grimaced. How could he explain the magnitude of the philanthropist's misconception—and his peril? "Mike, you're charged with a capital offense. You need an expert criminal lawyer. I'm a lawyer, but all my professional practice has been before the Patent Office. I've never been involved in a criminal trial."

Dore laughed aloud. "Neither have I. We can learn together."

"No, Mike. I can't let you take the risk. I'll help you find an expert, a top gun in one of the high-tech crime firms.

Maybe we can get Maxeck, of Shapiro, Dewitt. Or maybe even Olliver, of Cherryholm, Foster. They—''

"I don't want them, Quentin. I want you.''

Oh Lord, groaned Thomas. He shielded an intense and growing conviction. *Michael Dore is crazy.*

"I need you for special reasons,'' signaled Dore. "You're not just an ordinary psi, Quentin Thomas. Very few psis have your telekinetic ability. You may have heard of Professor Siva?''

Thomas replied carefully. "Just what they said on the casts.''

"The news was essentially accurate. Siva was to have been a prime factor in our Lamplighter Project. To make a long story short, when we lost Siva, we came to you. Your psi is approximately equal to Siva's. You both have a four- to five-kilometer control radius.''

Thomas waited uneasily. Where was this going?

Dore continued. "We can enhance that ability, multiply it.''

"Make it stronger?''

"Possibly. But mainly we extend the operative distance. We stretch your present range of a few kilometers out to many millions of kilometers.''

"You're not making sense.''

"I guess not. I can't tell you everything just now. It would be too dangerous for you. But I'll tell you in good time.''

Worse and worse. "No. I have to get back. I have a heavy docket with PSI.'

"Forget PSI.''

"But—''

"Henry Wright tells me you have a daemon.''

More little surprises. And a rush of sudden comprehension. "You own PSI.''

Dore nodded.

The lawyer shrugged. Locked in. "There's still a question of trial site. I recommend a change of venue. You certainly don't have to be tried here on Luna. Your alleged crimes took place on Earth. You can get a fair trial in any one of a dozen Federation High Courts there, from

Auckland to Zurich. They're all overloaded. On Terra, you can stall this thing for months. But if you do nothing, you'll have to accept trial here in Lunar Court. And I happen to know that the lord chancellor has a very light load. He's just finished a piracy case. He would probably get to you in a few days.''

"That's fine with me. It's got to be here. I accept that. In the first place, I don't think I would be able to get off the moon alive. I'm actually safer right here. In the second place, here *you* are, Quentin-with-the-daemon. You have one of the highest psi potentials in the solar system. I won't bother you with the details of our search. Aside from poor Siva, there appear to be only five psis worldwide with your telekinetic ability for electron and nuclear control. One of these is a little four-year old girl; one is a deaf-mute. One is in a nursing home. One—or two, depending on the point of view—is—or should I say are—an unseverable set of Siamese twins. In the group next below yours there are a couple of dozen possibles, but only one can visualize a U–235 atom, and none is a lawyer.'' He continued, choosing his words slowly, as though summing up for a difficult pupil. "Don't you see? I needed a lawyer with a scientific background—which you have. I needed a lawyer with an extremely high nuclear psi registry. But even beyond that, I needed to be able to get that lawyer here. The guillotine got you in. They let you in because they needed you to assemble it. They didn't realize you were also a lawyer. Nor did they realize you would be bringing in a device that would save my life.''

"The guillotine—will save your life?''

"Ironic, isn't it?''

"Incomprehensible might be a better word.''

Dore grinned. "I know it all sounds very mysterious just now. But believe me, I do need your powers of psi, and your legal skills, and your scientific background, and of course, the thing you brought with you.''

The lawyer concentrated. His mind was back with the guillotine. Setting it up in the Rotunda. The bailiff was asking him about the key to that panel in the side of the platform. That was it. Not motors, not batteries. Those were in a different part of the subplatform. This panel opened to a secret compartment. And in that compartment nestled the device that Michael Dore supposed would save his life. He stared searchingly at the other. "Cut the nonsense, Mike. I have to know. If I'm going to represent you, I have to know everything. 'Deceive not thy physician, confessor, nor lawyer.' "

"Very good, Quentin. George Herbert, *Jacula Prudentum*? Yes, you're right, of course. All right, it's a psi-enhancer, and it's locked in that panel in the base of the guillotine. When the time comes we'll get it out, and we'll use it. Or, perhaps I should say, *you* will use it."

"To ignite Jupiter," finished Thomas numbly. "I'm expected to be the climax of the Lamplighter Project. You planned for me—or somebody like me—from the beginning."

"That's right, I did."

The admission was so artless, so matter-of-fact, so devoid of any confession of deception that Thomas found himself unable to protest. He took a deep breath. "Let's back up a bit. You said something about enemies—people who could be hurt if the Lamplighters succeed. I don't understand. How could anyone possibly be hurt by the Lamplighters?' "

Dore smiled grimly. "It's really quite simple. Let me explain. There's a practice in the stock market called short selling. Are you familiar with it?"

"I know the rudiments. Basically, I contract to sell you a block of stock for delivery at a certain future date, at a predetermined price."

"That's right," said Dore. "Add one very important fact: you don't yet own the stock. However, you fully expect to be able to own it by the time you have to deliver it to the new owner."

"And if the stock jumps in value," said Thomas, "the seller takes a loss and the buyer makes a profit. But if the stock collapses, the seller can buy his stock cheaply, and the buyer has to take it at the original contract price, which is of course much higher. The seller makes a bundle."

"Exactly," agreed Dore.

The lawyer frowned. Can this really be happening? he thought. He decided to state his surmise as a question. "Mike, are you telling me somebody is selling Lamplighters short, and to make sure they can buy in low at their contract date, they're deliberately trying to sabotage the project?"

"Yes," said Dore.

He might as well say the whole thing. "And if necessary, kill you?"

"Yes."

"Who are they?"

Dore shrugged. "Good question. I'm not sure. All we know at the moment is that they also own a big slice of Peace Eternal. We're trying to run that down."

The younger man thought uneasily of his fiancée. He said, "Of course, if the project succeeds, Lamplighters stock will go through the roof, and they will be ruined."

"Quite true. So you can see, they're highly motivated." Dore laughed harshly. "Actually, until recently the stock was losing points without any effort on their part. Lamplighters was selling at fifty-two before Dr. Siva disappeared. A week later it was thirty-two. Last Monday it was twenty-three. When my indictment was announced, it dropped to eleven. I do believe they had a hand in that. If I am tried and found guilty, the stock will disappear from the board altogether. The syndicate will be able to buy it for pennies. We think their futures price is about fifty. They expect to buy for pennies and to take fifty per share from their contracts."

"What kind of money are we talking about?" asked Thomas. "In the aggregate."

"Billions. They will make—or lose—billions. There's nothing in between."

Thomas whistled. "Small wonder they want to put you away."

Dore studied the lawyer's face. "But we're not going to let them. We're going to put *them* away, Quentin."

Are we now? thought Thomas. And just how are we going to do *that*? He tried hard to recall something from his course in corporation law about the risks of selling short, but all that he could dredge up was an ancient Wall Street jingle:

> *He who sells what isn't his'n*
> *Must deliver the goods or go to prison.*

Well, maybe. He sighed. It was just too remote, too unreal.

No matter. His psi perceptions were tingling. They were about to be returned with a jolt to a very real present.

He said, "I sense two men in the corridor."

"I've been expecting them. They are coming to arrest me."

The door crashed in. Two uniformed men with guns drawn stood in the entrance.

Dore chuckled dryly. "Oh, do come in, gentlemen. Don't be bashful."

One of the officers stepped inside and studied Dore and Thomas a moment.

"I'm Michael Dore," said the philanthropist, "and this is Mr. Quentin Thomas, my lawyer."

Well, there it was, thought Thomas. Willy-nilly, Michael Dore had a lawyer. Or, to put it another way, he, Quentin Thomas, had a client.

There was a whispered exchange between the two newcomers. Then one of them spoke. "Nobody said nothing about a lawyer."

"You have a warrant for *my* arrest, signed by his lordship, Martin Rile," observed Dore, "but that doesn't include my lawyer. You're not supposed to arrest my lawyer. If you're confused, you can call his lordship."

"I'm not confused," growled First and Foremost. "He can stay." He pointed a finger at Dore. "You come."

"Certainly." Dore flung a telethought back to Thomas. "Find out about the arraignment. If I know Rile, it could be as early as tomorrow morning."

"I'll check it out."

"Coif and robe in the hall closet."

"I'll find them."

After the three left, Thomas called inn security to repair and reset the broken lock in his client's hall door, and then he set off toward his own room.

So, he mused, Dore and the Lamplighters knew he was a psi. The more he tried to hide, the more he shouted, "Look at me!" Well, so be it. He was what he was.

He had read somewhere that evolutionary pressures would inevitably produce a new hominid species, people with extraordinary talents. The theory seemed to have a sound biological basis. Our first recognizable ancestors, *Australopithecus*, had been here for two million years. Then *Homo habilis* had been here for half a million. Next was *Homo erectus*, Java man, who had been here for a mere hundred thousand. He was a perfectly respectable ancestor. He built fires in stone hearths. He hunted horses, deer, rhinoceros, even elephants. He chipped stones to make cutters and scrapers. He was replaced by Neanderthal, who flourished for fifty or sixty thousand years. Neanderthal brought with him improved tools and hunting skills, and he dreamed of an afterlife. And then thirty-five thousand years ago came Cro-Magnon—modern man—*Homo sapiens*, the supreme hunter. The time needed to bring in the next species was growing shorter and shorter. So maybe, he thought, the time is ripe for me. Except I don't want to be the new hominid. I want to blend into the crowd. I don't want to be strange. I want to hide.

Back up. Where did those new species come from? Take Cro-Magnon, the first *Homo sapiens*. He came into a world peopled exclusively by Neanderthals. Did that mean the first *Homo sapiens* had a Neanderthal mother? Interesting question. Actually, it wasn't all that long ago that the first *sapiens* baby was born. Thomas thought back to that day. Or night. He tried to imagine . . . the infant *sapiens* bursting headfirst from the heaving, grunting body of a Neanderthal mother. The circle of old females watching, and slowly realizing in dismay that they watched the birth of a monster: hairless, flat-faced, no brow ridge, high vaulted forehead, weak-chinned, legs too long, arms too long. His neck is so weak he cannot lift his head. The newborn howls. The howl is all wrong. They look about for stones and clubs. But *she* sees, and she snarls and cradles him in her muscular arms. They back away. Tomorrow. Maybe they will kill it tomorrow. There is always tomorrow.

Ave Maria. Blessed be the fruit of thy womb. He had survived. And others like him. Proof? The current human race.

6
Nights in a Turkish Harem

Gentlemen of the shade, minions of the moon.
    —*William Shakespeare, Henry IV, Part I*

He sensed *intrusion* as soon as he entered his apartment.
Had they actually been inside? Very likely. Mentally he
shrugged. He wasn't in physical danger. Not just yet. They
were just looking him over. On the other hand, he resented
it. Well, let's see what they've done. He waved a hand to
turn on the entrance light. Yes, the mirror. He let his cranial
alpha-wave nets sift through the glass, and beyond. They
had gimmicked it. It was now a video broadcaster. He
smiled into it as he peeled off his jacket and loosened his
tie. He searched for the three critical nodes in the microscopic chip glued to the back of the glass. Yep. Have to
get back to you.

He passed on. A check showed that his holo-video, vi-
deophone, and even the computer terminal were tapped.
And now he had to make a decision. He could do various
things, or a mix of various things. He could leave these
insidious insecta in place, or he could destroy them, or he
could convert some of them to his own use. The urge to
focus his mental energies on their micronetworks was
strong, but he resisted it. He knew that Dore wanted him
to conceal his psi abilities for the time being. All right, he'd
go along with the deception. For now.

But that left the big question: Who had done this, and
why? He let the sensoria flow in from the things in the
room. He was getting a hazy picture. The second of the
two guards . . . one of the men who had arrested Dore? He

58

had been here. The wireman. A misnomer, since there were no wires. But who was Officer Wireman working for? Here the images grew even hazier. Things kept snapping in and out of focus. But there was something there—something that suggested a short, heavyset man, clad in some sort of black robe. Efforts to bring the picture in more clearly just made it worse.

He wasn't getting anywhere. He yawned, and realized he was tired. He wanted to get some sleep, but in four hours he had to be in court, and he had a lot to do before then.

First, he had to get a copy of the grand jury transcript. He let his mind rove along the circuitry of the terminal. Then down the power conduit. Yes, there it was, buried inside the wall. An inductor, transmitting automatically to a central location, probably right here in the inn. He took a bypass and went on down the line. After a dozen cross-overs he found the central data bank for the clerk of the court. With delicate, subliminal probes, he accessed the general file menu.

The system was about what he expected, with the standard code names, traps, and safeguards.

The usual invitation showed as words in his mind. "Please log on."

He signaled, "Log on."

"Password, please."

Interesting. The computer didn't want his name or his user ID. Just a password. The lord chancellor's clerk must feel very secure about the system. All right, Mr. Clerk, here we go. Let's call up your password. It will probably be something short, something you and his lordship and the rest of the staff can remember easily. The possibilities were numerous, yet not infinite. Just a question of running through all the permutations for two, three, four, and maybe even five letters. A two-letter word would have 26^2 possibilities—676, of which only a fraction would make a recognizable word. Three letters would give 17,576 possibilities; four, half a million; five about twelve million. Even as he was thinking this, he was running the spectrum. Click, and a beep. Very short, four numbers, each representing a letter: 4—15—18—5.

The computer was talking to him again: "Command."
"List," he replied.
The unit said:

Attorney Roster
Complaints Filed
Court Calendar
Petit Jury
Bail and Escrow
Grand Jury

That was it. He signaled, "Retrieve Grand Jury."
He got another list.

Panel
Foreman Election
Docket
Minutes

Minutes? Must be the same as transcripts.
"List Minutes," he commanded.
He got

People v. York
People v. Gafter
People v. Dore

"Retrieve Dore."
There was a perceptible pause. He read, "Password, please."
Ah, another. He ran through the permutations quickly. Another four-numbered code. It took a little longer. Must have started somewhere around the middle of the alphabet: yes, 13—21—19—20.
Click, beep, and . . . a charge-out indicator. The grand jury transcript for Michael Dore had simply been moved—taken away—transferred to another place.
And *hold*. He sensed a trigger. An invalid code number would flash an alarm. This time, he'd have to get the code word right the very first time. No millions of preliminary

permutations. One wrong entry and his lordship would materialize from somewhere in robe and slippers and unplug his entire data bank. Or he might even be frightened into deleting the Dore transcript altogether.

Well, all right, he could do it, with slow, subliminal touches, up and down the combinative scale. But that would take hours, and he didn't have hours. All he needed was one more word, probably a short one, a word known only to the chancellor and his cohorts. He thought back. What was that first word? 4—15—18—5: Aha! D—O—R—E. Fair enough! Next: 13—21—19—20—which was MUST. Dore must—*what*? Certainly a short word, easily remembered. WIN? His own personal hope, perhaps, but unlikely that of the clerical filing system. LOSE? Well, hardly that either. PAY? Didn't ring right. Go? Go where? SEE? Silly.

I'm missing something, he thought. And I suspect it's staring me in the face. Hmm. The horrid dominant fact, something I seem to have a mental block on, is that I brought a guillotine here. Before Dore is even tried, he is condemned. That's it.

He signaled to the computer: 4—9—5. DIE.

Click, beep, he was in.

He clenched his eyes shut tight to try to make his head stop whirling.

Well, at least he had accessed their game plan. He would soon know how they proposed to kill Michael Dore.

They?

They evidently included the lord chancellor. Good God! What kind of court was this?

He sat there, stunned, barely thinking, stumbling helplessly through the alternates. Maybe the chancellor didn't know. No. The chancellor had to know. Maybe it was some clerk's sick joke. No, he didn't think so. A simple million-to-one coincidence? Absurd.

Let it go. For now, anyhow. Maybe a quick read of the transcript would explain everything.

And so he began to read.

Very interesting. Apparently there had been only one grand jury impaneled within the last six months. And even more interesting, it had heard testimony on only one case and had handed down only one true bill: Dore's indictment. And then, as of yesterday, the grand jury had been discharged.

But everything was there. Thomas felt like Ali Baba in the thieves' treasure cave. He raced through the recorder's styling notes, then found the verbatim transcript of this unique hearing.

But he couldn't dig in just yet. He had to provide some entertainment for the bug on his holo-video. He would sit here and pretend to watch.

Holding the chancellor's circuit open, he sent a secondary probe into the index of items available on his video. There, a nice one. *Nights in a Turkish Harem*. He confirmed the selection into the video terminal. A listener somewhere was now grimly but impersonally noting Mr. Thomas relaxing in his room, watching an X-rated cassette on his holo. This might be expected to go on for a couple of hours, and then it might indeed repeat. Now, thought Thomas, we don't want that unseen audience suddenly to realize they have been deliberately put on the wrong track. We don't want them to jump to their feet with questions. No, we owe them a quiet, soothing, relaxing couple of hours. We will superimpose on the *Turkish Nights* track a gentle, barely noticeable, hypnotic cycle. Something that gradually bores, then deadens. Incoming sensoria will be gradually muted. Scenes become slightly out of focus, hard to follow. Motion slows. There is a sense of yawning. And gentlemen (one or more), I dearly wish I could join you, just drift away. Perhaps in an hour or so, I shall. Meanwhile it is just as well that nobody knows that counsel for the defense is actually on the case. And so he began.

He read, he recorded, his eyes widened. His mouth opened as though to shout a protest. Beads of sweat grew on his forehead.

Three witnesses had testified before the grand jury. The leadoff was a Dr. Zole, a nuclear expert, a former Lamplighter employee. He testified that the Lamplighter Project could never ignite Jupiter. (Hence, thought Thomas, Dore had taken lunar money and couldn't deliver, and under lunar law that was treason.) Then there was Furkas, Lamplighter ex-comptroller. He had provided some devastating information and records about Dore's continuing systematic embezzling program. And there was a dirty dalliance with Swiss banks. According to Furkas, Dore never had had any intention of igniting Jupiter. Ninety percent of the Lamplighter income had gone straight into Dore's pockets. (Hmm, thought Thomas. Who's lying? His gut reaction pointed to the ex-comptroller—a discharged employee out for revenge. But who knew for sure?)

Hold on. The people's prosecutor was talking to someone. Who? Great heavens! It was the judge, the lord chancellor himself. Of all people who ought not be present at proceedings of a grand jury, the chancellor was absolutely number one! Hah! He could hear himself now: "Move to dismiss! Quash the indictment! Improper conduct!" And where would that get him? He had no way of knowing. He strongly suspected they did things differently here.

Anyway. On with it. Who's next? Who is this? Hard to make out. Ah, here we are. It's going into a holo cassette. I'll be darned. The prosecutor and the lord chancellor are putting together an interrogatory for somebody named Boslow. Who's this Boslow? Why can't he show up to testify in person? Well, well. He's the resident manager of the Lamplighter station on Io. Interesting. He'll be answering questions in court from one of Jupiter's moons. How will that affect my cross-examination? Problems, problems . . . Io is forty light-minutes away.

Boslow—another ex-Lamplighter. So much for loyalty. But give the man A-plus for sincerity and conviction, because if Jupiter ignites in the next couple of days, Io vanishes in a puff of smoke.

Michael Dore, he thought, can you really do that immense thing? I wish I could believe you. And if you can't perform, can I still save your remarkable hide? I wish I knew!

Who's next? Jarvis. Of course. Director of the Lunar Geologic Survey. He'll testify as another nuclear expert. He's the chap who's looking for water, with his seismic probe. I wish him luck. Seems reasonably honest. Probably not much we can do about him.

And so, he thought, we approach the end of the transcript,

and we find some very interesting concluding lines.

Chancellor Rile: Any more, Mr. Vulpin?

People's Prosecutor: Nothing further at this time, milord. That gives us four for treason. We need only two.

Chancellor Rile: You've ordered the machine?

People's Prosecutor: Yes. Actually they came to us. They offered a special deal. We can try it out before we decide.

Chancellor: They'll let you do that?

People's Prosecutor: We have it in writing. It's due on the shuttle tomorrow.

Chancellor: All right, go ahead. You can arrest him as soon as the shuttle is in and schedule the arraignment for the next morning.

Next morning? thought Thomas. That was—now.

For a long time he just sat there, pensive, immobile.

So it was all arranged. Give Dore a fair trial, then chop off his head.

Why? Who says? What great obstacle does he represent to—to *whom*? Who are the players in this deadly chess game?

Why did J. Henry Wright give me a one-way ticket?

He sat back in his chair, thinking.

What did it all add up to? He didn't know.

What did this strange, very improper colloquy between the lord chancellor and the prosecutor for the people imply? He didn't know.

Was there any chance all this could be simply some trivial differences in the lunar and terran judicial systems?

No.

Is Michael Dore a liar, knave, fool, charlatan, thief?

No. Wait. Back up. Fool, maybe, to be so rich, and to let himself get into such a mess. Fool? No, don't decide yet. Defer judgment on "fool." If *he* is, so am I.

Back to basics. Who is this man Martin Rile? He recalled rumors in the legal community that the lord chancellor was a rich man, with powerful friends, national and international, and had simply bought his judgeship. The required hearings in the U.N. had taken less than an hour. Thomas had known very little about it, and up to now had cared less.

He had seen pictures of the chancellor in the *Bar Review*: overshot brows on a fat red face, the brow tips daggering up satanically.

And in total opposition, that other stranger, Michael Dore. He too was certainly a man of great wealth and many worldly contacts. Surely he should be able to protect himself. And yet here he was, in prison, with his neck at risk. How had it happened? What could possibly save the man? Did he have an ace in the hole? A secret weapon?

That thing in the base of the guillotine? A psi-enhancer, he called it. He thinks I can use it somehow. How? What does he expect of me? What *should* he expect? I don't even know myself.

Grimly, Quentin Thomas pondered his next step. Should he put this record on a printer? Dangerous. Might reveal that he was a psi—in fact, a very high-level psi. He knew that the time had not come for such revelation.

There were no immediate solutions. He didn't want to think about it anymore. Not of Dore, the Lamplighters, the lord chancellor, the guillotine.

He just wanted to think of Nadys.

Just the other day, Nadys in the rec room of Patuxent Haven. He had left her pensive and wondering, wondering whether to accept him permanently. Why couldn't she make up her mind? He found her indecision mildly disconcerting. Was there something basically wrong with him? He didn't think so. She was so damn independent. Was she afraid she'd lose her identity if she changed her name to Mrs. Quentin Thomas? No sweat, he'd said. Keep your name and be happy. We'll get the words said over us, but you can keep on being Nadys Blanding. Actually, there are advantages in not changing your name. Think of the computer screwups you won't be causing with a new name . . . phone book, payroll, pension, insurance, auto registration, all that stuff.

What was the big hangup? They loved each other. He knew it, she knew it. What else was there? He exhaled a long windy sigh, and relived that last embrace at the Haven, in front of God, closed-circuit TV, and a dozen fascinated residents. Her nipples had hardened against his chest, and her pelvis writhed against him like an uneasy volcanic caldera. And he recalled something else. That entry in her Haven dossier: T—July 27. Just exactly what did *that* mean? It was all moot, of course. She'd be out of there before he could return to ask. Forget it, he told himself. You've got some very pressing problems right here, and you've got to attend to them quickly and with some measure of competence.

And he needed rest. So how about a short nap? He set his mental timer for sixty minutes and eased back in the recliner, thinking of Nadys.

He loved to recall that famous first weekend in Los Angeles, when they were making discoveries about each other.

They had gone for a morning stroll on the boardwalk, and they had wandered into a gypsy hall. Everything was automated. Intrigued, they chose adjoining booths, pulled the curtains behind them, and put coins in the slot.

In the semi-dark, someone had spoken to him in metallic, yet seductive tones. "Hi there. Let's get right to it. Just think of me as The Voice. What's your name?"

(From hidden speakers, he judged.) "Quentin Thomas."

"Ah, a professional gentlemen in his late twenties. Unmarried. If I'm wrong, don't worry. Are you still with me?"

"Yes."

"That's fine. If this is going to work, you'll have to cooperate."

"Okay."

"For starters, how about a little walk in the Viennese countryside?"

"All right."

A pan-holo scene began to form around him. He was standing on the side of a hillock looking across a green valley toward a cluster of buildings. "What's that?" he asked.

"We're in the Vienna Woods, and you're looking at the hunting lodge and guest cottages of the last Austrian emperor, Franz Joseph. The estate was called Mayerling. Do you know the story?"

"Well, a little."

"Go on," said The Voice.

"In the upstairs bedroom of the main building, Crown Prince Rudolph shot his mistress, Marie Vetsera; and then himself. Apparently they planned it that way."

"Some say one of the great love stories, paralleling Abélard and Héloise, Romeo and Juliet . . ."

He shrugged. "I know all that. Franz Joseph ripped out the interior of the lodge and converted it to a convent, where the Carmelites still pray daily for Rudolph's soul. *He* was buried in state in the cathedral, but Marie was tucked away in the cemetery at the Heiligenkreuz Monastery, and forgotten."

"Not completely forgotten. You and I remember her."

"I suppose. But what's the point of all this?"

"When Rudolph shot Marie, she was holding a rose. When her uncles came for her body, she was still clutching it. It was recovered and has been preserved."

"So?"

The center holo showed a long-stemmed rose resting in a transparent plastic case. Thomas watched the lid slowly open, like a book cover. He had the impression he could reach his hand into the holo and touch the petals. Someone had done a remarkable restoration.

"There is a very faint residual odor," intoned The Voice. "Not everyone is able to detect it." The sentence ended in an upward inflection. It was really a question.

So, he sniffed. "I detect . . . something. Geraniol? Citronellol? Or their esters? A mix, I think. Ah, of course. Attar of roses. Some of these essential oils are detectable in parts per billion. Many of them are pheromones . . . sex attractants. Hmm! Fascinating." Actually, it was an exact duplicate of Nadys's very subtle scent. He was greatly intrigued, but he was damned if he was going to tell this soulless computer.

"Fascinating, Mr. Thomas? Yes, but not surprising. Our nasal epithelia are equipped with a million olfactory cells per every one and a half square inches. Our memories for odors are much better than for sounds or pictures."

Ah! He thought he had it. This computer had no sense

of odor, no olfactory faculty, none at all. It was *suggesting* to him (or to his subconscious mind?) that he was going to detect whatever odor was most important to him at the moment. Marvelous!

"Ready for more?" asked The Voice.

He replied quickly, "Go ahead."

"Study the rose, please."

He concentrated on the fragile exhibit in the holo.

"Our rose," said The Voice, "bloomed in the late nineteenth century, and since then it has of course faded a bit."

"Not much, though," said Thomas.

"What color do you see?"

"Red."

"Let's try a color check. On the right you will see a spectral section, ranging from violet down to red. Would you please stop the pointer when it reaches the shade of red you see."

He did as requested.

"Ah," said The Voice. "Six hundred and eighty microns. A brilliant scarlet."

"So it seems."

There was a pause.

"Well?" he asked warily. "Where do we go from here?"

"I'm afraid I have been somewhat devious with you, Quentin Thomas."

"I suspected as much. But please explain."

"There was no odor to Marie's rose. None at all. Only lovers can sense an odor."

"So you say. And I suppose it wasn't a *red* rose?"

"No, it was not," said The Voice. "It was a rather simple rose, *Rosa lutea*, native to Austria. Originally it was yellow. The years faded it to ivory."

"But lovers perceive it as red?"

"Quite so, Mr. Thomas."

The lawyer grinned and shook his head in mingled admiration and disbelief. "Are we through?"

"Almost. We have been recording your alpha, beta, theta, and delta waves as integrated in your occipital area. In addition to these waves you appear to have others. We are not familiar with these, and did not use them. The traditional cycles have permitted us to construct the face of the woman you love. We will now show that face to you.''

And there it was: Nadys's face. Of course. He burst out laughing. And just then, in the next booth, peal after peal of uncensored chortles floated up. Evidently *her* program had served up *his* face.

For an additional coin you could get a four-color print-out—which they each did. He framed hers and hung it over his bureau.

It was a beautifully engineered con game. When a couple came into the hall, the programs probably automatically took note. But the rest was marvelous. The analytic work on the odor and color of that rose was superb.

"What did The Voice ask you," he demanded as they left.

"Oh, some silly stuff about the Danube."

"The Vienna Gambit, Variation F, for Female."

"Yeah."

"*An der Schoenen Blauen Donau.* You said it was blue."

"Something like that." She was vague. She wasn't going to admit anything.

"It's really brown—quite muddy."

"And it's none of your damn business."

Oh, Nadys, Nadys, Nadys . . .

Smiling, he slept.

7
The Arraignment

O! swear not by the moon, the inconstant moon.
  —William Shakespeare, Romeo and Juliet

Thomas found the people's prosecutor, Harry Vulpin—
identified by black-trimmed green robe—waiting outside
the courtroom door. He introduced himself.

Vulpin stared at him in uneasy disbelief. "Who did you
say?"

"Quentin Thomas, for the defendant."

"But—"

"Is there a problem, Mr. Vulpin?"

"No, of course not. It's just that you're not of record.
Somehow I had the impression Mr. Dore would handle his
own defense."

"He hired me just before his arrest last night. I'll enter
my appearance when court convenes."

"I see. Ah, when did you come in, Mr. . . . ah . . ."

"Thomas. Last night."

"Through . . . ah . . . proper channels?"

"Yes, of course." Thomas smiled faintly. "And with
the guillotine."

"The . . . guillotine?" Vulpin's face twisted into a puzzled frown. Finally he rearranged it into an icy smile. "Yes,
I see, I see. Of course. Welcome to the case, Mr. Thomas.
And if you'll excuse me, I think I'd better send a note into
his lordship." He turned away and scribbled something,
which he handed to his clerk, who trotted around the corner
and disappeared.

Thomas was vaguely amused. Somebody was going to

catch it. Who was going to blame whom for letting the wolf into the fold? Except that he was no wolf, and certainly these characters were not innocent little lambs. He had already decided that he didn't like the prosecutor. There was something oily, sly, serpentine, in the way the man spoke and moved. So what? Vulpin probably detested him equally. Perhaps even more so.

The bailiff unlocked the doors from the inside. Thomas, Vulpin, and a couple of dozen spectators crowded in. Counsel passed on up the aisle, through the bar, and to their respective tables.

A door opened in the far end of the courtroom. The bailiff (now in red and green livery) entered, scanned the room (like a pilot fish preceding a shark, thought Thomas), tapped his staff on the floor, and proclaimed: "All rise. All who have business in this assizes of the Lunar Court draw nigh and you will be heard by the lord chancellor, the Honorable Martin Rile."

The lord chancellor in a flurry of ermine-lined crimson silks was right behind the bailiff.

Thomas jerked. So *this* is the arbiter of justice who files his records under "Dore Must Die." He also sensed that this was the creature responsible for bugging his room. And that was still a puzzle. Were *all* newcomers routinely investigated? Aside from knowing that he brought in the guillotine, the investigators could have had no prior inkling of his association with Dore. They had no way of knowing he would contact the man. Even *he* hadn't known that, not until he opened the door to Number 41. Very strange.

He remembered now the armed guards and the lines at customs. He had wondered at the time. Lunar Security was checking out everyone. They had whistled him through as a special case, because he rode a deadly horse. They were watching for anyone who might help Michael Dore. He suspected that his room was not the only one bugged. Every newcomer probably was equally honored. And he further surmised that, had they known he might appear here to defend Dore, he would have been returned on the same shuttle that brought him in.

Who was doing this? Obviously the chancellor and the

prosecutor were involved. But why didn't they come out in the open? Probably because of the rows of cameras in the mezzanine. Under the watchful eyes of six billion viewers these men had to produce at least the illusion of a fair trial.

So be it, he thought. We'll go through the motions, play to the galleries, see where it takes us.

With a wave of his hand, his lordship muttered into the audio, "Be seated."

As the chancellor eased himself into his great plush chair, the visiting attorney studied the would-be executioner closely. The man pulled a flimsy tissue from somewhere, blew his nose with assurance, and dropped the tissue into an invisible receptacle. Thomas suspected that his lordship had been attracted to this place because his gross weight was manageable in the reduced gravity. He could hardly blame him for that. However, there seemed to be an unfortunate side effect: The dry air had apparently activated the judicial nasal passages, so that the judge had to blow his nose periodically.

The jurist looked down at Thomas. It was a strange look, and the lawyer was unable to analyze it. He sensed several things: surprise, contempt, cruelty, high intelligence, diamond-hard determination. It all seemed to add up to a certain evil integrity. That look said to Thomas: Dore Must Die, but I'm so smart I can kill him within the rules.

Well, milord, thought the lawyer, maybe you can, and maybe you can't. That's what this trial and several holo cameras is all about, isn't it? He looked around. Quite a few spectators in the back, though the benches were by no means full. And only two or three crews in the mezzanine media boxes. It's just as well, he thought. Things will pick up when the trial is called, and that's (he hoped) at least a couple of weeks down the road.

As he turned back, he noted that the chancellor was squinting at him again.

The lawyer readily sensed how the judge must regard him: a trespasser, an interloper, a fly in the soup, a pothole of unknown depth in the judicial highway. The jurist probably wanted very much to have the bailiff eject this dubious intruder, but was constrained by those two or three cameras looking down at him. So his lordship would make the best of it. Thomas could follow the clicking mental gears. All right, let Dore have his lawyer. That'll show the world that we are fair and reasonable, that we follow precedent, that we give him his day in court. In the end it's all the same: We'll kill him.

The chancellor turned away and spoke to the bailiff, who said something into his portable communicator. The jailer will now bring Michael Dore up from his subterranean cage.

Yes, there was activity behind the witness chair. And Dore, manacled and chained, emerged with two guards. He winked at Thomas. His keepers led him down to the defendant's table, where his chains were removed. He rubbed his wrists, then shook hands with his lawyer. The guards stood behind the table, out of Dore's immediate peripheral vision, yet very much present.

"Are you all right?" Thomas asked quietly.

"Yes, of course. Best night's sleep I've had in weeks."

Enjoy, my friend, thought Thomas. You might not have many more.

The clerk announced, "Docket Number 13, People against Dore, arraignment."

Thomas adjusted his wig, rose and straightened his robe lapels.

So did Vulpin. "Harry Vulpin, prosecutor for the people."

"Quentin Thomas, for the defendant."

The chancellor looked down at Thomas. "You are of course a member of the bar, Mr. Thomas?"

"Yes, milord. The District of Columbia. Also Maryland and Virginia. And I am admitted to practice before the Federation Supreme Court."

"Very laudable, Mr. Thomas. But those are all terrestrial fora. They have one pole star, and Luna has quite another: Zeta Draconis, to be astronomically precise. Indeed, some of our procedures have been described as draconian. Terran courts have their rules, we have ours. Put bluntly, things are different here. We tend to cut through a lot of red tape."

Things certainly are different here, thought Thomas. He nodded politely.

"Let us proceed," said his lordship. He motioned to the bailiff, who called out, "Michael Dore, hold up your hand."

Thomas spoke quietly to his client. "Rise and hold up your right hand."

Dore flowed to his feet with smooth dignity, held up his right hand, looked the lord chancellor firmly in the eye.

The judge glared down at him, then began reading from the CRT inlay in his benchtop. The audios picked up and magnified the grim whisper. "Michael Dore, you stand indicted in a true bill given by the grand jury sitting at Lunaplex, for that you have conspired to prevent the completion of that endeavor known as the Lamplighter Project . . ." His lordship had to stop a moment and get his breath.

Thomas watched this with interest. The judge was so fat—about three hundred pounds Earthweight, guessed the lawyer—that there wasn't much room in that mass of lard for lungs. Or heart. It was going to be an interesting trial.

His excellency was reading from the screen again. ". . . as forbidden by Article 5, Section 8, Subsection K, Treason by Embezzlement. How say you, Michael Dore, guilty, not guilty, or *nolo contendere*?"

"Not guilty, your honor."

The litany and response were older than the Wars of the Roses.

From the corner of his eye Thomas noted that a faint smile flickered around the edges of Dore's mouth. The lawyer winced. We are in enough trouble, he thought without antagonizing Sir Blubber.

"The defendant pleads not guilty," rasped the judge. "So recorded. Trial set for—"

Thomas was on his feet. "Milord, before we proceed to the question of trial date—"

"Yes, Mr. Thomas?" The chancellor was annoyed.

"Will the court entertain a preliminary motion?"

Rile frowned. "Make it fast."

"Thank you, milord. I move to quash the indictment and to dismiss the case."

The judge's eyes opened wide, but for just a moment.

Then they sank back into cheek-flesh. "Indeed, Mr. Thomas? On what ground, pray?"

"According to the minutes of the grand jury, an additional person was improperly present during much of the grand jury proceedings. That's a clear violation of the common law requirement of secrecy and freedom of the grand jury from outside influence."

The chancellor stared suspiciously down at Thomas.

He's wondering how I found out, thought the lawyer. Rile thought his private data bank was totally secure. But now he's wondering . . . counterspies?

The judge temporized. He addressed the people's prosecutor. "Mr. Vulpin, do you have an opinion about this?"

The prosecutor rose and fluffed out pale cadaverous cheeks as he answered. "I certainly do have an opinion, milord. An extra person at the hearing? No actual harm is alleged. Surely a trivial irrelevancy . . . a harmless informality. The motion should be denied."

The chancellor nodded. "I quite agree. Irrelevant. Motion denied. If that's all—"

"It's not all. I have another motion, milord."

"Another?"

"I move that your excellency recuse himself, in that *you* were the extra person in the grand jury hearings."

The little eyes narrowed again, but his lordship recovered quickly. "We must be reasonable, Mr. Thomas. I'm the only judge on Luna. I *can't* recuse myself."

"Then I move for a change of venue."

"Denied. And no more motions, Mr. Thomas. We really do have to move along. Trial . . . let's see. How about . . . tomorrow morning?"

The lawyer caught his breath. "*Tomorrow . . . morning?*"

"Do you have a hearing problem, Mr. Thomas? Tomorrow morning."

Thomas's mouth dropped. "But . . . I met my client only yesterday. We need time to consult, bring witnesses in from Earth, check records, take depositions. We need time to prepare a defense!"

The lord chancellor smiled bleakly. "The court owes your client a speedy trial, Mr. Thomas. It's in our Lunar Constitution.'' He tapped the CRT inlay in his benchtop. ''Ah yes, here we are: 'In all criminal prosecutions the accused shall enjoy the right to a speedy and public trial . . . ' '' He looked up in triumph. ''Verbatim from the Sixth Amendment to your own American Constitution, Mr. Thomas. Oh, you'll have plenty of time. You can do a lot in twenty-four hours.'' He looked over at the other table. ''Mr. Vulpin, are *you* ready?''

''Yes, milord.''

''Well, there you are, Mr. Thomas, we're all set. It would be a travesty of justice to delay further.'' He peered severely at counsel for the defense. ''Is something troubling you, Mr. Thomas?''

''Milord, I do have a procedural question. How can trial begin when the jury hasn't even been impaneled?''

''A *jury*, Mr. Thomas? You want a *jury*?''

''Yes, milord. And with respect, milord, the Lunar Constitution states—and I quote: 'The right of trial by jury shall be preserved.' Also taken verbatim from the American Constitution,'' he added coolly.

''I know that, Mr. Thomas. Very well, then. You shall have your jury. And since you're in such a hurry, we'll just use the one left over from our previous case.''

Thomas hoped his dismay didn't show. ''No *voir dire*, milord? No challenges, even for cause?''

''No, that won't be necessary.'' The chancellor was thoughtful. ''That's all very well for a terran court, but here it's a luxury we can rarely afford. You see, Mr. Thomas— and I'm happy to explain this for the record''—here he looked up toward the cameras—''every citizen legally residing in Lunaplex is exempt from jury duty. It's our law. We draw our juries from transients. We persuade our visitors to serve. Twelve regulars and one alternate.''

''But—!'' protested Thomas.

''No buts, counselor,'' admonished the lord chancellor. ''True, we give you a mixed bag, but they're all free from local prejudices, false impressions, and bias. So consider yourself fortunate. In any case, it's our law. And if that's your last objection—''

Thomas was hyperventilating. He would have liked to

quit, forget the whole thing. But he couldn't. He had to force himself to function. He croaked: "Bail, milord!"

"*Bail*, Mr. Thomas? *Bail*, you said?" The tone indicated that the lord chancellor thought Thomas was out of his mind. Thomas thought of Oliver Twist, asking for more porridge in the workhouse, and the overseer's incredulous "*More?*"

"But your honor, the Lunar Constitution states that—"

"—'excessive bail shall not be required,' " finished Rile cheerfully. "I know. I wrote it. Lifted it right out of the Eighth Amendment of your American Bill of Rights. On the other hand, Mr. Thomas, you must realize that your client is charged with a capital offense."

"I know that, milord, but—"

"And you must also know that he is a rich and powerful man. He could vanish the moment he steps outside this courtroom. He could hide in a hundred places on and off Luna. Indeed, I am informed, reliably, I think"—here a nod to the prosecutor, who gravely nodded back—"that a Lamplighter courier ship presently stands in orbit, ready to abduct the defendant and spirit him away."

"True?" whispered Thomas to his client.

"Partly. They're there, standing out on my orders. However, Vulpin has served a court order on the Port Authority to forbid landing."

Thomas turned back to the chancellor. "All that may be true, your honor. On the other hand, Michael Dore has led a blameless life. He hasn't even got a vehicle or waste cite. He is a well-known businessman and philanthropist with strong ties to the community."

The prosecutor looked over at Thomas and grinned. The chancellor seemed to have taken over Vulpin's lines with gusto, and the prosecutor was not about to interfere.

"Well, now, Mr. Thomas . . ." The chancellor leaned forward as much as his barrel shape allowed. "How much money do you think would guarantee Mr. Dore's presence at trial?"

"Try a million," whispered Dore.

"One million libras, milord."

Something ghastly, something that might have been a sort of chuckle, rattled out over the audios. Thomas realized that the lord chancellor has laughed. "Make it a billion, Mr. Thomas."

The lawyer gurgled and turned pale.

"Take it," whispered Dore.

"You'll have to make it *all*—not just ten percent."

"I can do it. It'll clean me out. I'll have to sell a stack of securities."

"Maybe not. It'll be up to the financial officer. He'll probably take a contingent assignment. If he's agreeable, it can all be handled by electronic transfer, and you'll be out in an hour or so."

Thomas addressed the bench. "One billion—agreed, milord."

Even his lordship seemed momentarily impressed. His eyes, nearly submerged in the quicksand of his upper cheeks, flashed, then closed to a fine squint. "Mr. Vulpin?"

The prosecutor smirked "Satisfactory, milord."

And now, thought Thomas, if Michael Dore is kidnapped and is never seen again, who gets the billion libras? Something about that in the Rules of Court. Yes, now I remember. Fascinating.

On the other hand, if Dore shows for trial, he will be condemned and executed.

Interesting alternatives.

The lord chancellor spoke into his audio. "Mr. Thomas, Mr. Vulpin . . . some intriguing procedural points have been raised by counsel, and we have, I think, made final disposition of these questions. In all fairness, I will outline now what I perceive to be the paramount issues. Mr. Vulpin, you should bear in mind that the basic issue is treason. You will need two credible witnesses to the same act of treason as committed by the defendant. Breach of promise to ignite Jupiter by the appointed hour, or impossibility thereof duly demonstrated, may be considered treason."

And now he turned stern eyes toward the defense table. "Mr. Thomas, you keep talking about dismissal. I will tell you what you need for dismissal. You need two things: First your client has to cause Jupiter to ignite. This must occur no later than tomorrow afternoon at five o'clock—seventeen hundred hours, Lunar Time. Second, the evidence of ignition has to be absolute. This court has to see your new sun shining there in the heavens, eyeball to eyeball, as it were. No theory. No holo newscasts. No rumors. No hypothesizing on the witness stand. *I have got to see it.*''

"But milord," protested counsel for the defense, "we're all underground here. Even if Jupiter ignites, you won't be able to see it directly. Your requirement of visibility—"

"Careful, Mr. Thomas. If you keep contradicting me, you'll conduct this trial in irons. *That's all. Adjourned.*'' He banged his gavel. The bailiff dismissed the court.

Two guards escorted the prisoner and his lawyer to the financial office, where Dore signed holding forms for trust accounts in half a dozen terran banks. An hour later they emerged and walked out into the Rotunda.

They got into the two-seater autocart at the head of the cart line.

"Got any money?" asked Dore.

"No problem." Thomas found a thaler and dropped it in the coin slot. The Plex grid lit up. His client leaned forward to punch "A-A," but the lawyer laid his hand on the other's arm. "Wait—"

Dore froze into silence.

Thomas wondered whether he was being childish. Was such super-caution really necessary? Maybe he was developing a case of galloping paranoia. No matter; you're dead only once. Very carefully, he began his probe of the circuitry.

Curious . . . very curious. The first fork off to the right was supposed to take them to the inn. But this little devil had been hard-wired to skip that fork and take the next one, a branch corridor that led out to— "What's 'W'?" he asked tightly.

"Waste," said Dore. "General sewage and garbage processing. There's a series of reservoirs . . . treatment tanks." He paused and chuckled wryly. "*Oho.* My bail is forfeit if I don't show tomorrow morning. Forfeit to whom? Who gets it?"

"Rile gets a third, Vulpin a third, the rest is divided among the members of the jury. And how can you laugh?

Good God, man, it's not a question of a little overnight kidnapping. They're trying to *kill* you.''

"I know. This is the third attempt. Just amused by the monotony. Well, do we walk, or can you override their program?"

"I can override; but would that tell them something we don't want them to know?"

"No, I don't think so. They'd just assume their wireman fouled up. If we walk, *that* might tell them something."

"Fine. We override."

As they set out, Thomas scanned the Rotunda quickly but thoroughly. Not much of a crowd—perhaps twenty people, coming, going, stopping, talking in little clusters. No one seemed to be paying the two litigants any particular attention. But that didn't mean anything, of course. The wireman could be there; he could be any one of them. Or (and this seemed fairly likely to Thomas), the conspirator could be long gone—waiting for his quarry at the "W" turnoff.

The lawyer clenched his teeth. "Let's get out of here."

8
Peace Eternal

An evil man cannot bring peace
to earth or moon or star.
   —Kadi Naipul, "Forebodings"

That evening they sat in Dore's suite, communicating by cranial transmission.

"You mentioned earlier that your enemies held equity in Peace Eternal," said Thomas. "Is there any real connection with you personally, or with the Lamplighters?"

"I'm convinced there is a connection," said Dore, "although I must confess we haven't found out exactly what it is. We've studied P.E. in depth. We've infiltrated them, we've pretended to be applicants for residence in their resorts. We still don't know anything for sure. It's . . . frustrating. Would you like to see a typical case history?"

"Sure."

Dore pushed a cassette in the holo viewer and pressed a button in the arm of his chair. The holo switched on. "There's the administration building for the Atlanta Haven. It's midmorning. A bus is arriving. About thirty people get off, mostly middle-aged and elderly. A few younger candidates. Some intend simply to look around, but most have brought suitcases, and they are going to stay. No problem about space. There is always plenty of room. Here's a lady driving into the parking lot in her Iacocca. Let's follow her inside. P.E. looks for hidden cameras, of course, but my agent fooled them." The next scene was an interview room. "They check you out. You can't join the ranks unless the government pays or unless you can prove assets of a least one hundred thousand libras.''

The lawyer made a brief mental calculation. "That seems fair enough.''

Dore smiled. "That's what the newcomers think. Let's zoom in on the interview. Our agent is ostensibly a recent widow. She's grief-stricken. She wants to retreat from life. She's trying to find out if this is the way to do it.

"Her interviewer is made up to look a bit like her alleged late husband. For this we let them 'steal' photographs and background tapes. They try to keep the resemblance low-key, just close enough to create a favorable subconscious impression. This rogue is one of their best. Listen . . .''

". . . yes, Madame Bucher. We take over all your burdens. Here, you can rest. You will have no financial concerns. We furnish everything: food, clothing, cottage, medical care, entertainment. Here, nothing can hurt you, nothing can cause you any pain. You will be surrounded by people who have your best interests at heart, people who love you.''

Dore chuckled wryly. "Damn, he's good! Watch this. He's pushing their contract across the desk to her. He hands her a pen. Suddenly she is embarrassed. She left her glasses in the car. No problem, he can send out for them. No, she knows exactly where they are. She doesn't want anyone pawing around in the glove compartment. She explains that she keeps letters . . . things . . . from her late husband there. She gets up. I'll be right back, she says. Watch his face. He retrieves the contract. He knows he's lost her. He's puzzled. He can't understand what he did wrong.'' Dore stopped the holo and looked over at the lawyer. "And *you* look puzzled, Quentin.''

"I thought I saw something—but, oh, never mind. Yes, I guess I'm puzzled as to why you are showing this holo to me.''

"Well, I can certainly clear that up. And then perhaps you'll understand who our enemies are. There are two basic systems for dealing with Earth's population overflow. My Lamplighter Project is one. Peace Eternal is the other. I propose to make Jupiter's moons habitable, available for a new wave of pioneers. Peace Eternal would solve population problems by mass murder.''

"Huh? What . . . ?''

"Mass murder. You sign up with Peace, and you're dead within a matter of months. And P.E. is the beneficiary of all your assets, or government subsidy. The death certificate reads cardiac arrest . . . cancer . . . pneumonia . . . whatever. No autopsies. The corpse is cremated. If the ashes are not called for, they are ground and mixed with ammonium nitrate and sold as a premium grade of ten-ten-ten garden fertilizer.'' He tossed the lawyer a paper packet. "Have a sample. Marvelous for roses.''

"Good Lord.'' Gingerly, Thomas put the packet aside on the coffee table. Thank God Nadys had not signed on as a permanent resident. Those empty chairs . . . She was safe for the time being, but he'd have to get her out of there the instant he returned, marriage or no marriage.

"Peace Eternal,'' continued Dore, "is becoming a world-wide political force. They are very rich and very powerful and very dangerous. Already they own city councils, governors, senators. They influence the election of prime ministers and presidents. It may be just a question of time before they put their own man in the White House. They fear only one thing . . .''

"The Lamplighters?''

"Ah, my boy, you're getting it. Yes, they fear the project. If I can bring it off, the population problem is solved for centuries. P.E. loses their political backing. Suddenly their murders are no longer socially beneficial, but criminal. Their personnel will begin to go to jail. One by one, their centers will close. The whole filthy scheme collapses.''

"So it's up to you and the Lamplighters?''

"Exactly. If I can stay alive for just one more day, we will bring it off. Their first three attempts to kill me were all rather bumbling jobs. All by Peace, of course. But they're getting better. This new one, my trial for treason, is much better planned. Legal murder, you might call it. It's almost certainly organized by the prime mover in Peace. The *gris éminence*, if you will. Probably the majority stockholder and the chief executive officer.''

"And who is that?"

"I'm still trying to find out. Wright is working on it, back home. He has to be careful. Digging into Peace is a very risky business."

"Yes." Legal murder. Very neat. That would settle everything quite conclusively. He thought back to the holo. Something on the interviewer's desk? What was it?

Dore interrupted his thoughts, musing almost plaintively. "They are wrong, wrong, *wrong*. And we're right. I *know* we're right. Our entire moral ethos is based on one primary axiom: It's better to be alive than dead."

"Hard to argue with."

"But it's just an axiom, Quentin, something you take for granted without proof."

Thomas nodded.

The other continued pensively. "And lots of axioms have fallen by the wayside since the days of Euclid and Plato."

"But not this one!" Thomas looked at him sharply. "We're going to get you out of this. You've got to *believe*." But do *I* believe? he asked himself. Do I believe we're going to ignite Jupiter by five o'clock tomorrow afternoon? I'm not really sure. Do I believe this trial is a farce and that powerful men are using it to kill Michael Dore and the Lamplighter Project? Yes, *that* I believe. And who are these men?

"Run the tape back," he commanded. "Just the last thirty seconds, where it shows the desk, the man, the contract."

"Sure thing."

"Hold it. There."

"What are you looking for?"

"The man's nameplate. All you can see is 'DDER.' What's his full name?"

"Not sure I remember. Tony Something-or-other. Batter . . . Mudder . . . a prime scoundrel by any name."

"Anthony M. Kudder?" asked Thomas, with a horrid sinking feeling developing in his stomach.

"Hey, that's him! You know him?"

"He was the foreman of your grand jury."

Dore's mouth twisted wryly. "It figures. He's part of the gang. Does that mean Vulpin . . . Furkas . . . ?"

"Also working for P.E.? I don't know. But it's certainly possible." He thought to himself, and how about Rile? Sir Dore-Must-Die Rile? It was all beginning to come together. He wasn't sure he wanted it to. He wasn't sure of much of anything, except that the chancellor had laid down two requirements for dismissal—ignite Jupiter and show it to the court. He had made the statement in open court in front of the media and six billion viewers.

And that brought them back to the main order of business. "I'd like to review what I think will happen tomorrow," the lawyer said.

"Yes, of course."

9
Though the Heavens Fall

"Is there anybody there?" said the Traveler,
Knocking on the moonlit door.
  —Walter de la Mare, "The Listeners"

Thomas explained the highlights of the grand jury transcript. "They'll have four witnesses: Zole, who designed Arthur Clarke Station on Io. Furkas, your ex-comptroller. Boslow, who'll speak directly from Io station. And finally Jarvis, of the Lunar Geologic Survey."

"Let's take them one by one," said Dore. "Zole is a good man, honest, sincere, well-grounded technically in nuclear physics. He'll probably testify that the Lamplighter Project can't ignite Jupiter. Him, we can't do much about. Next—Furkas? He used to work for me. In fact, he was chief treasurer for Lamplighters. I caught him stealing, and I fired him."

"He seems to have some documents—signed by you— to show *you* did the stealing," countered Thomas.

"No. If they show that, they're forgeries. We'll have to find a handwriting expert—"

"Not likely. Rile would never let him in, and besides, there's no time. But maybe there's another way."

"Oh?"

"It involves the way the truth drug is used on cross-examination. Or rather *not* used. My department. I'll handle Furkas when the time comes."

"All right. Your department."

Thomas said, "So let's see where we stand. They'll probably use Zole and Furkas in the morning session, then Boslow and Jarvis in the afternoon.''

"Boslow, here? I thought he was on Arthur Clarke Station, out on Io.''

"He *is* out there. And that presents a problem. Vulpin signaled an interrogatory out to him day before yesterday. Boslow will come on line, in the courtroom holo receiver. He'll answer the questions in Vulpin's interrogatory, and he'll take us on a guided tour of the station. It will be very dramatic.''

"Neatly done. You have to hand it to Vulpin. But maybe we can give Boslow some questions, too?''

"Doubtful. Each question would require forty-five minutes out, forty-five back. No chance for a proper cross-examination.''

"I suppose not. So, what is Boslow going to say in his holo?''

"That he has made, and is continuing to make, on-site inspections of Jupiter, and that the Lamplighter Project cannot possibly ignite the planet.''

"And that's a treason count, isn't it? Not good, Quentin, not good at all. Even if you knock out Furkas, that still leaves Zole and Boslow, two treason witnesses, and they're not done yet.''

"I'll move to strike Boslow, of course, based on inability to confront, but I think we know by now how Rile will handle any such motion.''

"We can always hope. And that leaves Jarvis?''

"And he may be the most dangerous of all,'' warned Thomas. "He's the director of the Lunar Geologic Survey, and I understand he's highly regarded in the international scientific community.''

"Yes,'' agreed Dore. "He'll tell the truth as he understands it.''

"That's the problem. He'll testify as a nuclear expert, and he'll say the Lamplighter Project can't work.''

"Hmm. And another vote for treason. But no matter.''

"What do you mean, 'no matter'? It matters a lot.''

"Listen, my pessimistic young friend, it's not all that one-sided. We have resources. Remember? We can deal with all of these so-called nuclear experts. In a way, they're working for us. We're going to need some information from Zole for your efficient use of the psi-enhancer. He could turn out to be our best witness. At the proper moment, we'll get out the enhancer, and you'll use it plus Zole's data, and you'll ignite Jupiter.''

''You keep saying that. It's time you explained exactly what you expect me to do with your little magic box.''

''Fair enough. Let's go ultra-secret.'' Dore switched to a different, nearly subliminal cerebral wavelength and went into psi-pher. As the philanthropist explained, Thomas's eyes grew alternately wide and narrow as he oscillated between belief and disbelief.

The lawyer said finally, ''I don't know. I've never tried psi on anything so far away before. Jupiter is over forty light-minutes distant.''

''You can do it, Quentin. You *have* to do it.''

Thomas groaned. ''Let's say your enhancer actually works . . . I mean, that I am able to use it to project my psi out that far and blow the damn planet. That's only half of Rile's requirement for dismissal. We still have to show it— the new sun—hanging out there for all to see.''

''But how can he insist on *that*? That's impossible!''

''So is telepathic ignition of Jupiter.''

Dore looked startled, then he laughed. ''*Touché!* All right. But look, it's just a legal formality, isn't it? There must be some other way to satisfy those clowns that the planet has blown. We'll work it out.''

Famous last words, thought Thomas. He said, ''I'm going for a walk.''

''Be careful.''

''Don't worry. They always save the lawyers for the last.''

A few minutes later he found himself in the Rotunda, hands clasped behind his back, standing in front of the guillotine, and concentrating hard. Say we actually do ignite Jupiter with the enhancer, how then to demonstrate the planet glowing the open sky?

Nice question.

Can I talk Rile and/or Vulpin out of the requirement?
No.

Even if by some superhuman leverage of the enhancer he
could initiate fusion at Jupiter's metallic hydrogen boundary
and if by some miracle that was all that was needed to set
the giant planet afire, how was he going to show it to this
blackguard jurist? There was no way. It could be blazing
directly overhead, and it might as well be on the other side
of the galaxy. It would be completely invisible to the trog-
lodytes of Lunaplex. The moon village was completely underground. Well, not completely, perhaps. The Rotunda
dome stuck out a bit, of course, as did, he supposed, some
of the hardware of the lunar observatory, on the other side
of the moon.

Time and opportunity permitting, he could plant explosive charges in the courtroom roof, ignite planet and roof
at the same time, and demonstrate the new sun to judge,
jury, counsel, and client, all neatly dead and buried under
tons of shattered basaltic maria. He could almost hear the
air whooshing out through the great roof-wound, and irises
spinning shut all over the area in response to the sudden
pressure drop.

So now who was crazy?

Already, the place was getting to him. What about the
poor devils who lived here? What did they do when they
felt the rabbit-warren walls closing in? Did they come here
to the Rotunda and stare up at the translucent alabaster
panels of their dome? Their one link to sky and Earth? Or
did the dome frighten them?

As he lowered his gaze, a man walked past the fountains
and shrubbery, circled the guillotine, paused briefly as he
noted Thomas, compressed his lips with great disapproval,
and walked on into the Geologic Survey lobby. Thomas
recognized him from photographs. Dr. Jarvis, Survey Chief.
An expert witness for the prosecution. But why the heavy
displeasure? Something to do with the delay of Jarvis's
seismic shot? Most likely. Interesting. A shot on the other
side of the moon. Probably one of the biggest impacts on
the lunar surface in several billion years.

Very, *very* interesting.

He tries to recall PSI's seismic inventions, back on Terra. Different kinds of tremors, P waves, S waves. Various ways to detect. But all that was subtle, delicate stuff, mostly locating tunnels being dug under prison walls. On the other hand, the principles were basically the same.

The trouble with bringing down this dome was its great engineering strength. Domes were the final expression of architectural stability. Look at the magnificent domes of the ancient world: the Roman Pantheon, one hundred forty-four feet in diameter. The dome of Santa Sophia in Byzantium. The Taj Mahal. St. Mark, in Venice. All still standing. Only an earthquake could bring them down. And even then, it would have to be a special earthquake. Made to order, as it were. It wouldn't be called that here, of course. Here it would be a moonquake. And it would have to be very precisely structured moonquake. And what characteristics, he thought, would we require of this very hypothetical disturbance? He wished he dared call Nadys. She was a seismic expert, and she would know exactly what he needed. But that would tip off Vulpin right away. The oleaginous prosecutor would immediately sabotage the venture. He'd have to figure it out all by himself.

Tomorrow afternoon at five o'clock—seventeen hundred if one had a military mind—Jupiter would be directly overhead.

If Dore was right, it would be a new sun—distant but blazing. And would Dore win? No, Dore would still lose, at least here in court. Why? Because that brave new world would be invisible to Martin Rile.

Unless . . . unless . . .

He heard voices. A couple of nearby men were talking. That explained it. No, it didn't explain it. Because at this particular instant they were silent, and yet he continued to hear voices, exactly as if they were talking. Somebody was saying, " . . . Gagarin Crater . . ," Another voice: " . . . rather precisely on the other side . . ." " . . . antipodes, Dr. Jarvis?"

Hah! Exactly on the other side of the Rotunda stood Dr. Jarvis and another man. A reporter, Thomas surmised.

He was standing on one of the foci of a whispering gallery. Which very likely meant the dome, right down to the floor, was a nearly perfect parabola.

Ah, it reminded him . . .

He had once stood in a specific spot in Statuary Hall, under the dome of the Capitol, in Washington, D.C., and Nadys had stood in that other spot, meters across the Capitol Rotunda, and he had whispered to her, "I love you," and she had grinned. But then he had added, deadpan: "You have a gorgeous belly button and magnificent tits."

She had swiveled about in horror, then she had realized no one else could hear him. She thumbed her nose at him. Thus encouraged, he began, in businesslike monotone, a detailed description of her body, starting with the back of her neck, her shoulder blades, her spinal curvature. He was about to describe the dimples in her maxima glutea, when he saw that she was racing toward him. He fled through a side exit, a few steps ahead of her. He had turned and grabbed her on the British Stairs, where the redcoats had stormed in to burn the building in 1814. The troopers could have lit their brands on what passed between them then.

Another place.

Another time.

But there were similarities. And differences.

The dome of the Capitol consisted of iron gores riveted together. It was probably immune to earthquakes.

But *this* dome? It was built of individually cut translucent alabaster blocks carefully cemented together by suited men working outside in paralyzing cold and stunning heat.

What had Jarvis said so softly? Antipodes? When that Geologic Survey shot finally goes, does Jarvis get a series of compressive rings stretching up, up, girdling the moon, then shrinking, shrinking, as they begin to come together . . . *here?*

He had often wondered about the Old Testament account of the fall of Jericho. The Israelites had marched around the city for seven days (setting up a lethal resonance in the valley substructure?) and when the trumpeters sounded their continuing blast, the vibrations were no longer endurable. The walls came down. Maybe it helped that the doomed city sat athwart a fault as active as the old San Andreas? Who knows.

He looked up again. Such a beautiful dome. Will you, won't you? Come down, that is, so we can dance in a distant as yet unborn red light?

Dome. From Italian, *duomo*. The early Italian churches all had their big beautiful domes. They endured. Northward, in France, Germany, England, cathedrals soared skyward in lacy Gothic arches. And the higher they soared, the closer they got to heaven, the sooner they fell. Finally the flying buttress was invented, and that seemed to solve the collapse problem.

And the domes could care less. They just kept on enduring.

FIAT IVSTITIA ET RVANT COELI

Frustrating . . . and tantalizing . . . and . . .

Time to get back.

He felt a pang as he passed the French fountain. Poor dead thing. You should have stayed in Versailles. Will you ever receive the gift of life? Just a few make-up liters of water per day? Perhaps. Who am I to say?

And then the guillotine. Ah, ridiculous superfluity. But you got me here.

He looked up again. Wait . . .

Someone had said, "The moon rings like a bell." And that had been for a rather minor meteor impact.

He was getting the glimmer of an idea. There was something there, but not yet fully developed. He couldn't force it, but on the other hand he didn't have a lot of time. He would have to have the complete solution in mind by court time tomorrow.

He looked up into the dome once more, as though somehow the answer was written there.

FIAT IVSTITIA ET RVANT COELI

Let justice prevail though the heavens fall.

He knew that one. They had laid it on an old Roman, Lucius Caesoninus. Why do we have to go back to the ancients for our inscriptions, and in their original tongue, no less? What did the Romans do for *their* inscriptions? They quoted Homer and the *Iliad*, of course. And the

Greeks? They were fortunately excused. For them, there were no quotable ancients. So far as they could see, writing began with them. They never knew they stole it from the Phoenicians, who stole it from the Egyptians.

He looked up again. Try a slight twist: Justice prevails *because* the heavens fall.

What would it take to get the heavens to fall?

With his eye he estimated certain measurements of the great dome.

And now to get back.

He had gone about a hundred meters when he noted that a man was walking rapidly behind him. It made him uneasy. Considering the cart incident of the morning, he felt he had a right to be cautious. Perhaps he should have accepted Dore's offer of companionship. No, that wouldn't have worked. He had needed to get away by himself.

He let his mind flow into the brain of the following man. Yes, there was some surgical alteration there. Sections of cerebral cortex were hard-wired to elements of the inner ear. And those elements had also been altered. By means of tiny oscillators in each ear the Follower could send and receive electromagnetic radiation. Not uncommon. Thomas had heard about such modifications. Anything else? Yes. Surgical changes had also been made in certain tiny parts of the inner ear that control equilibrium. He had heard about that operation, too: It was supposed to result in immediate adjustment to lunar gravity. As he hastened his stride a bit, he realized that it might become important to recall the precise details of that elegant and subtle ear surgery. Adjunct to the ear's three semicircular canals (those primary elements for control of balance) one finds two tiny hollow sacs, the utricle and the saccul, each lined with sensitive hair cells and containing miniscule otoliths, or "ear stones." As we walk or stand or sit, the otoliths press against certain hairs in the utricle and saccul. If one leans forward, the otoliths press against other specific cilia, and those hairlets duly pass information back to the brain of the degree of inclination.

Without turning his head, Thomas let his brain waves explore the Follower's utricles and sacculs. The investigation confirmed what he thought he remembered. The ear stones—normally a simple, difficultly soluble form of calcium carbonate (rather like kidney stones)—had been replaced by tiny spheres of a special corrosion-resistant ferrous alloy. The substitution of the heavier metal pellets was supposed to accelerate the body's response to movement in the lower lunar gravity.

Possibilities? He seemed to recall something from an undergraduate biology course. Lobsters (and certain other crustaceans) have hearing apparatus remarkably similar to the human ear. In the lobster the ear stones were grains of silica, of course, not calcium carbonate. The students had replaced the silica ear stones with tiny flakes of iron. You could hold a magnet over Lobster 101 and he would suddenly think he was swimming upside down. He'd flip over instantly, and then he'd *really* be upside down. It was all a question of which cilia were being stimulated. The instructor finally had to hide the magnet. It was one of the few things Thomas remembered about biology. He still thought of the course as Lobster 101.

Possibilities.

But the ear alterations were not the only surgical modifications. The Follower had a very sharp, very long, titanium blade embedded in the muscles of his forearm. It was spring-loaded and could be sprung at will or by defensive reflex, like the talon of a tiger.

This citizen was capable of very unfriendly conduct.

Thomas squinted up ahead. Nobody up there. No pedestrians. No cart traffic. Where had everyone gone? And just when he could use some company.

The lawyer now had to do a bit of mental math. Would he make the A-A before he was overtaken? Maybe. He lengthened his steps.

The Follower broke into an easy jog.

Damn, thought Thomas. This is getting serious. Turn and have it out? Just as soon not. I think I can handle him, but you never know for sure. So why risk it?

He tried to break into a run, but it was clumsy, uncoordinated. His pursuer was now closing in with long graceful leaps—thanks to those metal otoliths, thought the quarry glumly.

Aha! Here comes someone! A rescuer? An audience, at least. Will the beast dare attack in front of a witness?

Oh Lord! No! No!

Too late.

The newcomer seized him in an iron grip, whirled him around in a mugger's special, forearm under his victim's chin, squeezing his windpipe. No need to put a hand over his mouth. Thomas couldn't get enough air into his lungs to utter a sound. All this creature needed to do was hold him immobile for a few seconds, until Follower arrived with his secret blade.

Quentin Thomas got his terror under semi-control. He ran his mind up and down the nerves of this man-vise. Yes, they were adrenaline-fed. By a tiny microchip implant in the occipital. This monster *thought* strength, and his adrenals released epinephrine and other goodies. His muscle power doubled . . . maybe tripled. His blood pressure increased, his spleen contracted and squeezed out extra blood, his blood glucose rose, his blood clotting time decreased. His pupils dilated so he could see better in dim light.

Nice, nice, thought Thomas. For soldiers in combat, for murderers out on a physical contract. On the other hand, it may be too much of a good thing. You like adrenaline, my friend? Glad to oblige. He blasted the man's microchip, and it in turn ordered the adrenals instantly to discharge all stored epinephrine and norepinephrine. Those remarkable hormones commanded veins and arteries and capillaries to contract . . . tight . . . tighter. The killer's blood pressure mounted: 200, 300, 400 . . . His cerebral capillaries were now popping and flooding his cortex. Pretty little blood puddles were suddenly materializing all over his brain. The mugger lost all muscular control, voluntary and involuntary. Thomas felt the iron arm dissolve and fall lifeless. Behind him, the attacker's body collapsed.

And here was Follower. The arm blade was out, but the wielder of this metallic death statement hadn't yet realized that he was now working alone.

Thomas closed circuits in the implanted oscillatory coils in the man's inner ear. Good. He was getting a nice magnetic field *above* those little iron otoliths, which now jumped *up*, convincing Follower's brain and all his organs and muscles that he was upside down.

Follower stumbled, fell, practically at the lawyer's feet. The eyes flailed wildly, searching for *up*, and for *down*. Thomas stepped aside. Follower grabbed frantically at his fellow thug, like a drowning man trying to hold on to a would-be rescuer. But there could be no rescue. Follower twisted his head around. The corridor ceiling was now "down" to him. Somehow, he knew he was floating on the walkway, which was now his ceiling. He couldn't understand how he came to be stuck to the ceiling. He was terrified. He knew he was about to "fall," and that the four-meter drop to the corridor ceiling would kill him. He held desperately to Iron Arm and began to sob.

And here were more running feet. Four men. A Security Patrol. Good or bad? wondered the lawyer. Safety in numbers, he hoped.

He was soon explaining. "Not sure exactly what happened, corporal. That one—he pointed to the Follower—"was holding that belly-sticker on this other chap. And then suddenly the big fellow just collapsed."

The corporal bent down and felt Iron Arm's pulse, looked at the bloodshot eyes. "Heart attack," he muttered. He called somebody on a wrist radio. "Fox here, Corridor 5 at sixty meters. Send us a meat wagon." He looked down in disgust at the Follower, and added, "With restraints. We got a primary claustro." He turned and studied the lawyer a moment. "Name?"

"Quentin Thomas."

"You're here for the trial?"

"Yes."

"A-A?"

"Yes."

"Thank you, Mr. Thomas. You'd better go on, now. We'll contact you if we need anything further. And I suggest you not wander about alone."

"Thank *you*, corporal. I'll remember that." He bowed and walked on toward the inn.

Should he tell Dore about this? He didn't want to. Why

worry his client? Maybe later, when (and if) things eased up a bit.

As he entered Dore's suite, the philanthropist looked up and smiled. "Your brow is still wrinkled. You must have had some heavy thoughts."

Thomas grinned. "I don't often concentrate. When I do, my brow gets all wrinkled, like a wadded-up piece of paper. It can be a task to unwrinkle it. I was trying to figure out how to make your ignited Jupiter visible to the chancellor."

"You're still on that kick? Well, how will you do it?"

"If we can do it at all, we'll need your psi-enhancer and some help from Dr. Jarvis."

"The Geologic Survey man?"

"Right."

"Well, I don't think we can expect much help from him. He hasn't forgiven us for holding up his seismic water shot. Remember?"

"I remember. Well, no matter. Let's review what we can expect to happen tomorrow. It will start with opening statements. Vulpin will lead off, then me. Then Zole, then Furkas, then lunch break. That's when we'll get out your enhancer." The lawyer went over every foreseeable step, pausing frequently for Dore's comments and suggestions. They quit after midnight, wondering what crucial points they had overlooked.

10
Opening Statements

Certain truths are examined best by moonlight.
    —Milton Fitzjames, Censored Fragments

Quentin Thomas and his client had breakfast in the Rotunda
Cafeteria. They sat at a table in the open area facing the
courtroom. To their right was the French fountain. To the
left, the guillotine. In the middle, under the dome, was
the rock. All dormant, waiting . . . for what? thought
Thomas. He watched the passersby. A bit of a crowd. They
were all waiting for the courtroom to open. The hall of
justice would not be able to accommodate all of these people.

Dore had already shooed away a couple of reporters and
cameramen. Perhaps he and Dore should have taken a table
inside. On the other hand, if assassins were loitering about,
they might be less likely to make another try in front of
reporters and cameras. Actually, Thomas didn't feel safe
anywhere anymore. Perhaps not even in the courtroom.
What lethal intellect lay behind yesterday's two attempts?
And why was that person or persons no longer content to
rely on murder-by-trial? Somewhere out there, in enemies
unknown, he sensed a growing indecision. He could not
understand it. The chancellor had permitted full media coverage, perhaps on the theory of trial of such importance
could hardly be concealed. The eyes of the world were on
this courtroom. Perhaps *that* was providing a measure of
stability and protection to Michael Dore—and to him.
Maybe. On the other hand, they (and who were *they*? Peace
Eternal?) still held all the cards. They controlled this court,

the prosecutor, the jury. They controlled (by injunction readily granted by the lord chancellor) all travel and all communication, into and out of the moon. They controlled—yet the control was flawed, imperfect: because he and Michael Dore were still alive. And that was so because *he* could control the flow of electrons along conductors. As long as he could do *that*, and as long as the media continued to cover the trial, he had a chance. It was ironic. He sensed that six billion watchers, a quarter million miles away, had more control over the lord chancellor than he.

He thought, none of this should be happening. Not this way, anyhow. Dore needed an entire team of expert criminal lawyers, not to mention a twenty-four-hour crew of bodyguards. This isn't for me. I ought to be back home drafting patents. Nadys and I should be . . . oh, hell.

And did any of this bother his client? He looked over at the philanthropist. Dore was having a second order of flapjacks and bacon. Thomas ordered a second cup of coffee. He hadn't touched his one meager croissant.

"Eat up, son," ordered Dore. "You can't face the wolves on an empty stomach."

How does he do it? thought Thomas. Why is he so confident? His great plan verges on insanity. Even if it works. Especially if it works.

They had been watching the bailiff and his assistants doing busy things at the guillotine. The crew was going to test it with a man-sized dummy.

"We shouldn't be watching this," whispered the lawyer. But they did watch it. They couldn't take their eyes away. The baliff pressed a button. The blade ran up the guides. Two men took the stuffed body and laid it facedown, neck in the notch. A woven willow basket waited under the head. Just the right size. A red index line had been drawn on the back of the thing's neck. Everything matched up nicely. Thomas touched his own neck, then noticed what he was doing, and jerked his hand away, with a guilty look at his client, who simply grinned and reached for the croissant: "If you don't want it, Quentin." The lawyer pushed the plate over.

"Patentable?" asked Dore.

"You tell me," Thomas responds dourly. It is historically inevitable, he thought. Rather like Dr. Guillotin, of French Revolution fame, who was responsible for the introduction and mass use of apparatus for the instant and theoretically painless separation of body and soul, and who was eventually served with his own machine. The most unkindest cut of all.

The crew now took the three cables, each terminated by a button. Thumbs on buttons, they awaited the bailiff's command. No one would ever know who was the actual executioner.

"Mark!" cried the bailiff.

The blade dropped. All they saw was a flash. They heard a snick. The head of the dummy jumped a little, then fell cleanly into the waiting basket.

"Very efficient," murmured Dore.

His lawyer was wordless. He thought, they plan to murder you in full view of several billion eyes, probably sandwiched in between detergent commercials, and all you can say is "Very efficient."

The bailiff locked the blade down. His helpers stuffed the decapitatee and the head into a waiting garbage sack. The three men left, going in different directions.

Thomas looked morosely at his watch.

"He's going to call the court. We might as well go on in."

"All rise," chanted the bailiff, and his lordship, Martin Rile, chuffed in and eased his great bulk into the black plush of his high-back chair. The jurist held something in his right hand. Thomas swallowed. Yes, it was the black cap. Rile would trade peruke for cap when he pronounced sentence of death. Not so fast, my venomous friend, thought Thomas. We're a long way from that. The lawyer took a deep breath and continued his inspection of this man who wanted to kill his client. He noted with interest that the judge was wearing a great deal of gold. Gold rings, gold bracelets, gold chains about his neck. Even gold earrings, for God's sake. (No bone sliver through the nasal septum, milord?) His lordship's cheeks were delicately rouged. He wore purple eye shadow. A black beauty spot adorned his left cheek. Of course, the trial was to be holoed, and of course this character intended to sparkle. Thomas looked overhead at the glint of lenses in the media boxes. And then to the rear of the courtroom. Already overflowing. It was going to be a circus, with a psycho ringmaster.

So it must be. The lawyer smiled grimly. The stock exchanges in New York (where it was six A.M.) would be closed today so that all Manhattan could see justice done in this quarter-million-mile-away room. As would the Paris Bourse (noon there) and the great London Exchange. In San Francisco and Los Angeles it was three A.M. and alarm clocks were buzzing. In Honolulu and Auckland they hadn't gone to bed yet, and wouldn't. In Karachi and New Delhi the sun was still high in the sky, and brown faces were locked in to communal holos. They would all assume that this archcriminal, Michael Dore, was guilty of blighting their lives, and the lives of their descendants, and indeed, the future of the human race, and they would all be determined to watch him get his just deserts.

And his beloved? Was Nadys up early in the rec room at Patuxent Haven, watching these ghastly proceedings, and planning some delicate hell for him because he had kept her in the dark? Peace! my darling, my luscious volupté. Be mollified—I'm much deeper in the dark than you.

And now the jury filed in. Twelve men, plus an alternate. And they all belonged to Rile and Vulpin. Gentlemen of the shade, minions of the moon.

"Hey! There's our old friend," observed Dore.

Thomas saw him right away: the last juror to enter. "Kudder."

"Tenacious Tony himself."

And now Thomas noted an interesting thing about the foreman. Kudder's jacket bowed out a little as he sat down, and the lawyer caught a very brief flash of metal: a handgun ensconced in a shoulder holster. And not just any handgun. It was PSI's Laser Model 95, available (he had thought until now) only to prison guards. It was named Model 95 because of its special circuitry. It shot a red laser beam out of a tiny sapphire cylinder with an efficiency of ninety-five percent, compared to five or ten percent for prior lasers. He had gotten a patent on it only last month. Was this to be the crowning irony? Shot with PSI's very own laser? Not if he could help it!

He rose as he called out. "Milord! May I approach the bench?"

The chancellor frowned, then nodded.

Thomas and Vulpin walked up together.

There was something about Vulpin's step, something confident and springy, that seemed to say the people's prosecutor already knew how this little preliminary confrontation would end. And that was very interesting, because Vulpin didn't yet know the nature of the upcoming objection. Perhaps Vulpin didn't have to be burdened with such trivia. Perhaps all Vulpin needed to know was that the dice were loaded, the deck was stacked, and there were two strikes on the batter before he even reached the plate.

The lord chancellor looked down at the visiting defender with puffy, indecipherable eyes. Thomas saw there an odd mix of amusement, annoyance, and perhaps just a trace of uneasiness. He knows, thought Thomas, that they tried to kill us yesterday. But why should he be concerned? Isn't that exactly what he's trying to do? Of course, here in his own courtroom, under scrutiny of the media, he'll try to aim at murder-by-the-book. He wants to look good. Is he running for governor? Senator? Perhaps even Federation president? That might explain it.

Thomas and Vulpin waited while his lordship pulled a scented tissue from a bench drawer and blew his nose in sonorous ritual. Thus cleared, his lordship could now focus on counsel for the defense. "What is it, Mr. Thomas?"

"I object to the jury, milord. It's not an impartial cross-section of the community. Mr. Kudder, for example, was foreman of the grand jury that indicted my client. He is obviously biased. And I speculate that all the other jurors were likewise drawn from the grand jury panel."

"You *speculate*, Mr. Thomas?"

"It seems a strong possibility, your honor."

"No need to guess, Mr. Thomas. Yes, they were indeed

drawn by impartial, nondiscriminating lot from the grand jury.''

''But, your honor . . .''

''They were the only nonexempts available,'' explained Rile patiently. ''Everyone else is a lunar or government employee or a medical or health aide. Can't help it, Mr. Thomas. Didn't I explain all this yesterday? Actually, you may consider yourself fortunate.''

''Fortunate?''

''These jurors already know a lot about Mr. Dore's treason. Alleged treason, perhaps I should say. They can reach a verdict much more quickly.''

They already have, thought Thomas. He turned and looked toward the jury box. His eyes locked momentarily with those of Anthony Kudder. The juryman smiled back at him. Rogue, growled Thomas mentally. He recalled lines from *Measure for Measure*.

> *The jury, passing on the prisoner's life,*
> *May in the sworn twelve have a thief or two*
> *Guiltier than him they try.*

This was surreal. It couldn't be real, even though it was being played out as real. He wanted to turn and scream to the cameras . . . to the entire solar system, that nothing here was real. But he knew he wouldn't and couldn't. He would finish this fantasy one way or the other. Still . . . He turned back to Rile and began feebly, ''But . . .''

The chancellor silenced him with a bang of the gavel. ''Opening statements. Mr. Vulpin?''

''Thank you, milord.'' The prosecutor waited a moment while his defeated rival returned to the defense table, then adjusted his wig, gave his robe an accusatory swirl, and launched his case by pointing a long bony finger at Dore. For a moment he was silent, holding the pose (Thomas assumed) in heroic tableau for the benefit of those holo cameras up in the mezzanine. (That picture, Thomas suspected, would appear in the *Peoria Populist*, the *London Times, Pravda, La Prensa*.) Then Vulpin began, in a voice so harsh that the visiting lawyer winced. ''Milord, gentlemen of the jury, that man, Michael Dore, already one of the richest men in the solar system, was not satisfied with what he had. His insatiable greed drove him to form an organization known as the Lamplighters, with the stated object of causing the planet Jupiter to ignite and make a second sun. When this occurred, the Galilean moons would warm up and become small, habitable planets. They would provide sufficient arable acreage to absorb Earth's population overflow for centuries to come. When would this happen? He promised it would all happen by five o'clock this afternoon.''

Vulpin was pacing slowly back and forth in front of the jury box. Some of the jurymen seemed to be watching him attentively. Some seemed bored. One or two seemed hypnotized, as though by the rhythmic sinuosities of a circling python. Thomas noted that Kudder appeared to be vastly amused by something. By what? Was it the too obvious theatrics of the prosecutor? The whole farcical trial? Or something beyond all that? No way to know just yet. It would all come out.

Thomas exchanged glances with his client. Dore just smiled. Thomas concealed his irritation. Not a smiling matter. No indeed. He wanted to remind the other that the execution would be held right here on the Rotunda, so his lordship could watch. And it would be done with a certain patent-pending, motorized, never-fail guillotine. Vulpin had spoken to him about it (with that wet, evil grin) this morning in the cafeteria anteroom. And with a leering twist of the knife: "Weren't you the attorney on the patent, Thomas? Not a conflict of interest, I hope?''

He blinked hard. He needed to concentrate, take careful note of everything that went on here, in this room. Everything that was said, everything that was not said.

One of the jurors with a language box hadn't plugged it in. And why should he bother? thought Thomas. He already knew how he was going to vote. What was the going rate for a lunar juror?

"To accomplish this," continued Vulpin, "Dore needed money—immense amounts of money. He had to build a fleet of special ships, to carry nuclear waste to Jupiter. He needed money to build an observatory station on one of the nearer Jovian moons. He needed staff in the overpopulated areas of Terra, to select emigrants. He needed many, many vessels to transport his human freight. He needed vast contributions from whole nations. Just last year, for example, he took one percent of the entire gross terrestrial product. He *took* that, milord, gentlemen. And then he deliberately sabotaged the Lamplighter Project. He deliberately saw to it that the giant planet Jupiter will not, *cannot* ignite. And meanwhile, where has the money gone? Those billions and billions and billions? Oh, of course, you'll find a few ships built and under construction. Indeed, one is in lunar orbit at this very moment, awaiting an opportunity to whisk this felon away. And of course there's actually a small observation station on Io. But the rest of the money? The rest you say? Where is the rest of the money? Who has it?''

The prosecutor turned away from the jury box. Out came the accusing finger again, like a flashing sword ready to deal with a fire-breathing dragon. "I'll tell you who has it. *He* has it! *That man*! The greatest cheat, hoaxer, swindler, charlatan, and mountebank ever seen on Earth or Moon! The people of Lunaplex charge him with embezzlement, fraud, and theft. And those are just the minor offenses. The big ones are treason and conspiracy to genocide. As consequences of his acts we count the eventual premature deaths of at least two hundred million human beings. Under our Lunar Laws, the penalty for treason is . . .''He paused, as though he could not bring himself (as a basically caring, civilized human being) to say the terrible word. The jury, as one man, leaned forward. The courtroom was suddenly silent. The lord chancellor paused in the very act of bringing a tissue to the baronial nostrils.

Dore looked at Thomas and winked.

"*. . . death,*" said Vulpin.

The entire human content of the great room relaxed with a windy sigh. The prosecutor put his hands over his eyes and bent back momentarily as though to shut out a vision too horrible to contemplate. (Nice touch, thought Thomas.) Finally Vulpin returned slowly to his table and sank wearily into his chair. He was drained utterly by his analysis of the terrible crimes of the prisoner. "That's all," he muttered.

The lord chancellor wiped his eye with a gold-lace bordered handkerchief. (Was he laughing or crying? wondered Thomas.) "Mr. Thomas?"

"Thank you, milord." He adjusted wig and robe and rose for his opening statement. He bowed gravely to the bench. "Milord." Then to the jury. "Gentlemen. I'll come immediately to the point. Mr. Dore categorically denies all charges. True, Lamplighters took in a great deal of money. But it was all well-spent. And it's true that Mr. Dore contracted to ignite Jupiter today. We admit it. But conspiracy? That's nonsense. If there's any conspiracy, it's by others, to prevent him from fulfilling his contract."

Vulpin jumped up. "Objection! Milord! Make him stick to the issues! What's this sudden reference to a third-party conspiracy? There's no truth in any of that!"

Rile laughed and glanced up briefly toward the mezzanine. "Truth, gentlemen? At this point, do we really know what the truth *is*?" Thomas sighed. He realized that the judge had been waiting for an opening like this, and wanted them to play the game for the benefit of the cameras, something to show that the contest would be conducted on a high intellectual level. "What *is* truth, Mr. Vulpin?" Thomas was surprised. He didn't know Rile read the Bible. And maybe he didn't. Quoting Pilate didn't prove anything.

Vulpin's mouth hung open, disorganized. He didn't know what was expected of him.

Rile gave up on the prosecutor. He was becoming petulant. "Can you help us, Mr. Thomas? What is this elusive commodity dispensed in the halls of justice? What is truth?"

Defense counsel shrugged. "Various possible definitions, milord." He stared coldly up at the little pig eyes. "Try this one. Truth: any proposition as to which opposition is currently ineffective. Example: Jupiter burning in the sky."

"Oh, nicely put, Mr. Thomas! Especially that part about Jupiter. We'll have to remember that." Rile motioned to the court steno, who had paused, bewildered, wondering how much of this was to go on the record. "Note it down, sir!" commanded the chancellor. "Truth is Jupiter burning! A sprightly aphorism indeed and especially applicable to the case at hand." He sat back. He frowned. "And with truth duly and accurately defined, including an apt examplar, let us get on with it. Are you done, Mr. Thomas?"

"No, milord, I am not done. My opening statement was interrupted. I have a few more words. Today, Michael Dore will cause Jupiter to ignite. It will hang in the overhead skies, burning, for all to see. That *will* happen, and when it does, that will be proof that Michael Dore is innocent of all charges." He sat down.

There was an uneasy silence in the courtroom.

The lord chancellor stared down thoughtfully at counsel for the defense. He looks like an assembly of very red, very ripe tomatoes, disguised as a judge under black robes, thought Thomas. The top tomato wears a wig and carries two blotches that might be mistaken for eyes.

Finally the lord chancellor cleared his throat. "Mr. Thomas, your statements far exceed the partisanship permitted an advocate. As you very well know, your client cannot possibly ignite Jupiter, today or any other day. Nobody can. It would take a direct act of God, a divine interference with the laws of physics, as it were, and that is not going to happen, and you know it."

Quentin Thomas sprang to his feet. "But that's the basic question, is it not, milord? You say I know it can't happen? With respect, milord, I know no such thing. No one here knows that Jupiter cannot, will not ignite by the appointed hour. Nor do *you* know, milord. Indeed, that's the precise issue for which defendant's indictment was laid." He concluded in a very loud voice: "*You cannot deny him his right to be heard!*"

A great buzz burst up from the audience. The chancellor banged away with his gavel, and the noise subsided. "Mr. Thomas," he said slowly and carefully, as though choosing his words for the law reporters, "This trial, in all its phases, will be conducted with decorum and courtesy. You are not allowed to scream at me. You are not allowed to contradict me. You are not allowed to tell me I do not know how to conduct a simple one-day criminal trial. I hereby hold you in contempt, fine to be determined at trial's end. You are a disgrace to the bar. Further, I intend personally to petition your disbarment."

"*Milord . . . !*" He groaned inwardly. Could this lunatic get him disbarred? Just now, it seemed quite possible.

"Sit down, Mr. Thomas. Mr. Vulpin, call your first witness."

11
One Sure for Treason

Chanting faint hymns to the cold fruitless moon.
   —*William Shakespeare, A Midsummer Night's Dream*

Vulpin grinned at Thomas as he turned to the witness row.
"I call Dr. Zole."

A tall bearded man emerged from the seats, was duly
sworn in, and walked up to the witness chair.

Vulpin breezed through the preliminaries and got down
to business.

"Are you presently employed, Dr. Zole?"

"No, I'm between jobs."

"What was your last employment?"

"Project Leader, Lamplighters. I reported directly to Mr.
Dore."

"How long did you work for Lamplighters?"

"Three years."

"And what were your duties during that time?"

"I had special ships built to handle nuclear materials,
and I organized pickup of nuclear waste from several
hundred points around the world—Terra, that is. I nego-
tiated contracts with several governments."

"Contracts to haul away their nuclear wastes?"

"Yes. Not everything, though. We didn't bother with
waste having a half-life measured in hours or days. Argon
41, for example. It dropped to one-millionth of its initial
level in thirty-two hours. Nor did we bother with iodine
131, which became substantially harmless after six months.
Things like that, we never transported. We took only the
high-level wastes, with half-lives of decades or more: stron-

tium 90, cesium 137, and especially plutonium 239, the deadliest of all.''

''And then what?'' asked Vulpin.

''We freighted them in to Io. There they were repacked into one-way rockets and shot into the Great Red Spot. On Io there was a certain preferred order by which the incoming material was sorted and loaded into the rockets. All this was done by radio-controlled scoops. After the rocket was loaded and sealed, it was just a question of waiting for the Red Spot. When it showed on Jupiter's western horizon, the rocket was locked into the computer clock. Minutes later, the rocket motor fired, and the bird was on its way.''

''Then all this came to an end. For you, I mean.''

''For me, yes.''

''Mr. Dore fired you?''

''Not actually. We parted by mutual agreement.''

''What do you mean?''

''He kept insisting on a specific ignition date of—today, actually. I told him it was impossible. But he said he could do it. He seemed quite certain. He honestly believed he could do it. I felt I had to resign. He didn't object.''

Vulpin folded his arms across his chest and walked over to stand squarely in front of the jury box. He tossed the question over his shoulder: ''Dr. Zole, in your professional opinion, is it possible for Jupiter to ignite? To turn into a small second sun?''

''No, it is not possible. Not today. Not this century.''

''Explain, please.''

''Jupiter has plenty of hydrogen, which it could burn if it were indeed a sun. But big as it is, it has only one-fiftieth the mass of the sun. That's not enough to give it the internal pressure and temperature it must have to start hydrogen fusion. For that to happen, it would need a mass at least four times its present mass. It can never achieve such mass.''

''What temperature would be needed to start hydrogen fusion?''

''At least ten million Celsius. The sun, for example, has an internal temperature of about forty million.''

''Is it your testimony, Dr. Zole, that nothing can be done by human beings to convert Jupiter into a small sun?''

"That's correct. Jupiter is nothing but a big planet. It will always be a big planet. There is nothing we can do that will make it anything else."

"Thank you, doctor." Vulpin turned to Thomas with arched eyebrows and a faint smile. And now a bit of protocol. "Will learned defense counsel cross-examine Dr. Zole?"

Thomas rose and bowed. "Yes, Mr. Prosecutor. We propose to cross-examine the witness."

The lord chancellor looked down on this with great interest. Meanwhile he blew his nose on a perfumed tissue.

Vulpin said, "Does counsel require that a truth drug be administered to the witness?"

"The defense expects that Dr. Zole will cleave to his oath," said Thomas. "We waive the truth drug."

All had gone as everyone had expected.

Vulpin shrugged. "Your witness."

Counsel for defense approached the podium. He exchanged noncommittal stares with the witness. He began slowly, almost contemplatively. "You say we need a temperature of ten million to start hydrogen fusion?"

"Yes."

"And the sun has forty million?"

"Yes."

"The sun is hot because it fuses hydrogen?"

"Basically, yes."

"You mean it's really a bit more complicated?"

"Well, overall the solar mechanism is, one carbon 12 reacts with four hydrogens—protons, that is—to make one helium 4 plus radiation."

"And even *that* is somewhat oversimplifying it, isn't it, doctor?"

"Of course. You want the whole thing?"

"Yes. Just to help the jury understand what's going on."

"Well, in the sun, the cycle starts with one atom of carbon 12 and one proton—a hydrogen atom, that is. They fuse and give one atom of nitrogen 13, which decomposes to carbon 13 plus a positron and a neutrino. Carbon 13 plus proton then gives nitrogen 14, which soon fuses with proton to give oxygen 15, which loses a positron and a neutrino to give nitrogen 15, which fuses finally with one proton to give carbon 12 and helium 4. And then you start over.''

"Ah, thank you, doctor. Very concisely put. You start out with carbon 12, and you have carbon 12 left over. Carbon 12 is sort of a—what do you call it?"

"A catalyst."

"Yes, catalyst. That's the word. It isn't used up, but it's absolutely essential to the reaction?"

"Quite so."

"You can't fuse hydrogen without carbon 12?"

"I wouldn't go that far. Actually, any of the isotopes in the sequence would serve the same function."

"And these are—?"

Dr. Zole ticked them off. "Well, in order of their entry into the mechanism, nitrogen 13, carbon 13, nitrogen 14, oxygen 15, nitrogen 15."

"Would you agree with me, Dr. Zole, that carbon 12, plus each and every one of those isotopes, is included in one or more of the shipments of nuclear waste deposited on Jupiter by the Lamplighter Project?"

"Yes. But they're all useless."

"Because the temperature is too low?"

"Exactly."

"But aren't there other nuclear processes that don't involve carbon 12, and which would provide plenty of heat?"

"Not sure what you mean."

"Well, let's consider the Big Bang. You're familiar with the Big Bang theory."

"Of course."

"Did the Big Bang make any carbon?"

"Probably not."

"But stars were born, and they radiated light and heat?"

"Of course. Oh, I see what you're driving at. They used the proton-proton fusion mechanism. Do you want me to go into that?"

"Please do."

"Two hydrogen atoms fuse to give deuterium plus an electron and a neutrino. Deuterium reacts with another proton to give hydrogen 3—tritium. Two tritiums fuse to give helium 4 and two protons, and you start over. At one million

Celsius the proton-proton mechanism predominates; above
that, say at ten million degrees, the carbon 12 cycle is the
main line. After the early stars made a little carbon 12,
they—"

"Let me interrupt, doctor, just to clarify . . . did I understand you to say you can start the stellar process by
proton-proton fusion at a temperature as low as one million
degrees?"

"Well, yes, but even *that* is way above anything on
Jupiter."

"What *is* the temperature on Jupiter, doctor? Or should
I say *in* Jupiter?"

"It varies, depending on where you measure it. At the
cloud tops it registers about minus one hundred thirty degrees Celsius. At the center we estimate thirty thousand.
That's a bit warmer, but not nearly hot enough to start any
kind of nuclear reaction."

"Can't the nuclear wastes provide a certain amount of
local overheating?"

Dr. Zole shrugged. "I don't know."

"So you can't deny the possibility?"

"The trouble is, counselor, any local heating would be
instantly dissipated. Jupiter is an enormous heat-sink."

"But for a small, finite time, temperatures of the order
of one million—or even ten million degrees—might result?"

"Oh, I suppose."

"And in contact with the planet's liquid metallic hydrogen?"

"Wild speculation."

"Do you say it could not possibly happen?"

"The idea is . . . bizarre . . ."

"But if we had sufficient nuclear fission at just the right
spot, that would give a temperature of at least one million
for at least a brief instant, wouldn't it?"

"Possibly."

"And if that occurs at the hydrogen layer, what would
happen?"

"I don't know."

"If you don't know, you can't rule out ignition, can you, doctor?"

"This is ridiculous."

Vulpin rose. "Your honor, Dr. Zole has said he doesn't know, but Mr. Thomas keeps boring in. He's harassing the witness. Make him switch to some other area."

"Move on," commanded Rile.

"Nothing further," said Thomas.

"No redirect," said Vulpin.

"You may stand down, Dr. Zole. Call your next witness, Mr. Vulpin."

"Courage, my boy," whispered Dore.

What to say? thought Thomas. That's one sure witness for treason. They need just one more, and then it's the guillotine. I've got to do better.

12
Pananias

Thou liar of the first magnitude.
  —William Congreve, Love for Love, Act II.

Vulpin turned to the witness row. "I call Reginald Furkas!"

A small, pasty-faced man hurried up between the counsel tables, carefully not looking at Dore.

"My ex-treasurer," whispered the philanthropist. "He stole, and I fired him."

The witness was sworn in. Vulpin asked the routine preliminary questions: name, residence, age. And then came the exhibits. First, the clerk sticks little blue decals on each sheet, "People, For Identification No._____." Then he filled in the blanks, P–1, P–2 . . .

The lord chancellor and defense counsel were given a set of copies. Dore flipped through them, then whispered to his lawyer. "Forgeries."

"Every one?"

"Each and every."

Vulpin got down to business. "Mr. Furkas, I show you People's Exhibit Number 1 for identification, and I ask whether you can identify it."

"Oh, yes, sir. It's a memo from Mr. Dore to me."

"Saying what?"

"He asked me to set up a secret Swiss bank account for him."

"Thank you. I show you now People's Exhibit Number 2 for identification, and ask you whether you can identify it."

"Another memo from Mr. Dore. He ordered me to divert

115

ninety percent of all Lamplighter funds, present and future, to his Swiss account.''

A buzz in the courtroom. Rile banged his gavel.

''And did you make these diversions, Mr. Furkas?''

''Oh, yes, sir.''

''Now, Exhibit Number 3. What's this?''

''A Lamplighter financial report. He asked me to conceal all diversions.''

''*He?*''

''Mr. Dore.''

''He required you to file a false report?''

''Yes, sir.''

Document after document.

Vulpin grew sadder; he was almost compassionate. Finally, ''Mr. Furkas, why are you here now?''

''It was too much. He had to be exposed. I told him I was going to report him to the authorities. He fired me, of course. And he threatened me. I feared for my life.''

''But you courageously came forward.''

''Yes, Mr. Vulpin. Out of a profound sense of civic duty.''

''Of course.''

''I may vomit,'' said Dore quietly. Thomas put a hand on his client's arm.

Vulpin said, ''I offer in evidence these Exhibits, P–1 through P–34.''

''Objection,'' said Thomas. ''Defense is entitled to cross-examine prior to the proffer.''

Vulpin shrugged. ''All right. I'll save the offer until after cross.''

And now to the question of truth drug. This time the protocol would be different. Vulpin knew this, as did his lordship, the jury, the courtroom audience, the court steno, Michael Dore, bailiffs, medic (waiting over there with his kit), and certainly counsel for the defense. Thomas alone, however, knew in what precise respects the little drama would vary from the routine scenario.

''I presume learned defense counsel wishes to cross-examine Mr. Furkas?'' asked Vulpin.

"Yes, Mr. Prosecutor, we propose to cross-examine the witness."

All of the lines were straight out of the Book of Procedures.

"Does counsel require that a truth drug be administered to the witness?" continued Vulpin.

"The defense expects that Mr. Furkas will cleave to his oath," replied Thomas smoothly. "Nevertheless, to protect both the people and the defendant, and intending no disrespect to Mr. Furkas, we will ask that Mr. Furkas accept the truth drug provided to the medical clerk by counsel for defendant, or, alternately, that the testimony of Mr. Furkas be stricken in its entirely." (For Thomas, too, knew the Book.)

"Of course," said Vulpin agreeably. "For the record, Mr. Furkas, we have analyzed the truth drug offered by the defense, and we confirm that it fully complies with the specifications of acceptable medications. Will you accept this drug?" He nodded to the witness.

"Oh? Oh, yeah, sure." Furkas giggled nervously. "Bring it on."

"Yes, we'll do that. But first . . ." Vulpin hesitated, as though he was having a sudden, probably trivial, after thought. "Your voice sounds a bit harsh. You've been testifying at some length. Is your throat dry? Would you like a drink of water before Mr. Thomas begins his cross-examination?"

"Water? Well—"

"You would like a glass of water, wouldn't you?" Vulpin threw the words of the witness individually, like rocks. It was not a question. It was an order. The prosecutor poured a glass of water from the carafe on his table.

"He's prepping him for your cross." whispered Dore. "That glass is loaded with Pananias. You could see the white powder before he poured the water in. It's supposed to neutralize truth drugs—especially our Veritas."

"I know."

"Can't you stop him?"

"I could. But I don't want to."

They watched Vulpin hand the glass over to the witness, who drank it down noisily.

"*Now* what?" whispered Dore. He was puzzled and indignant.

"Patience," hissed Thomas. He looked at his watch. "It's our best chance. There's a thing about Pananias that's not generally known. If it isn't followed promptly with a truth drug, it begins to decompose in the low pH environment of the stomach. The decomposition products include some very subtle, very potent analogs of Veritas!"

"Good God!" breathed Dore. He began to relax. "How long does it take?"

"About five minutes."

"Five minutes. Can you stall them?"

"Watch me!"

Vulpin now nodded to the medical clerk, who approached the witness with a glass of cloudy liquid.

And now Thomas seemed to come to life. He leaped to his feet. He cried out, "Milord! Defense changes its mind! *We waive truth drug!*"

Dore half rose, as if horrified. Thomas pushed him down. The medical clerk stopped, stumbled. A little liquid splashed from the glass. Vulpin was on his feet. "I object!"

Thomas grinned. "Under the rules of this court, the cross-examiner is entitled to waive. We waive. Surely, milord, the learned prosecutor may not be heard to complain that his witness will not tell the truth without being drugged? And indeed, milord, for us to *insist* on a truth potion might well be considered an affront to the court. If I may quote your lordship." Here he picked up a brochure from his table. "For the record, this is from the Lunar Guidebook. Your lordship is being interviewed. You say, 'I have a special witness chair. It encourages truth . . . '"

Rile stared down at him, perhaps, thought Thomas, trying to figure out whether and how to object to himself.

Meanwhile, counsel for the defense continued in cheerful flood. "And look at Mr. Furkas, your honor. Have you ever seen a more honest face?"

Furkas smiled beatifically at the lord chancellor. With just a touch of rouge, thought Thomas, those cheeks would fit nicely among the cherubim on the ceiling of the Sistine Chapel.

Rile shot a mean hard look at Furkas, then back to Thomas, where he saw only boundless innocence. The jurist bit his lip. Thomas read the expression clearly. Rile was trying to figure out what happens when a witness takes Pananias and doesn't follow up with a Veritas chaser. The chancellor cast a quick, surreptitious glance up at the media alcoves in the mezzanine. He'd like to declare a thirty-minute recess and figure this out, thought Thomas. But he doesn't dare. And now who's he glaring at? Vulpin? Vulpin's no help, you juridical jackass. Your friend the prosecutor doesn't even know there's a problem. You're on your own. You've got to chance it.

"Waiver granted," mumbled Rile unhappily. His lordship blew his nose in a gesture of irritation.

The medic retreated. Counsel for the defense advanced.

Thomas picked up Vulpin's last batch of exhibits and approached the witness. "Mr. Furkas, I show you People's Exhibits P–1 through P–34, which in your direct testimony you identified as Lamplighter records implicating Mr. Dore in setting up secret bank accounts, and showing receipts of large sums of money from the governments of the United States, Japan, Soviet Russia, Britain, France, and many other countries, all going to those secret bank accounts. Do you recall these exhibits?"

"Yes, sir."

Thomas took a quick look at his watch, then studied the ex-accountant for a moment. One hundred and thirty seconds. Theoretically that was all it took. With no Veritas to activate it, Pananias should now be starting to run in full reverse. Look at the unequal pupils, faint haze of perspiration on the brow and upper lip, rapid respiration.

He thought, I still can't see the final victory Dore is so confident about, but at least we will have a few laughs along the way.

He grinned. Furkas, you lying microbe, you are dead meat. He says, "Mr. Furkas, my next question is very important. You're going to answer truthfully, aren't you?"

"Oh, absolutely, Mr. Thomas."

Thomas said, "Mr. Furkas, all of these exhibits are forgeries, aren't they?"

"Yes, sir."

All sounds came to a grinding halt. A sudden silence
seized the great room. It was so profound it was almost
audible. It throbbed.

Thomas noted that the court reporter was flicking his right
ear and looking puzzled, as though he heard something, but
nothing that made sense.

Then, with a highly audible intake of breath, Vulpin was
on his feet. "Objection! Objection!"

And now a scrabble of voices was heard in the audience.
It rose quickly in pitch and volume. Rather like an ancient
rocket blast-off, thought Thomas. Individuals were standing
here and there, and their neighbors were pulling at them
and yelling.

Rile broke out of his shell of frozen disbelief and reached
for his gavel. Pow . . . bang . . . bing . . . He went up the
scale.

And finally, silence again.

But still Rile said nothing.

Thomas wasted no time. He decided to construe the judicial inaction as overruling Vulpin. He faced Furkas. "All
your previous testimony was a pack of lies, wasn't it?"

"Oh, *no,* Mr. Thomas."

"What?" It was Thomas's turn to be shocked.

"I *did* give my right name," explained Furkas virtuously.

"Ah, so you did." (Did his relief show?) "Now then,
Mr. Furkas, who paid you to forge these records?"

"I don't really know, Mr. Thomas. It was all done over
the phone. A man said he would deposit ten million to my
account if I would make up these records and testify at Mr.
Dore's trial. Half and half, that is."

"Half and half?"

"Five million when I agreed to the deal, five million after
Mr. Dore's conviction and execution."

"And they really paid the first five million?"

"Oh yes. They were very nice about it."

"Objection!" cried Vulpin. "Counsel is deliberately
trying to confuse the witness. Mr. Furkas doesn't know

what he is saying. The people move that all of this cross-examination be stricken. Mr. Furkas is incoherent. He is obviously ill. Forgeries, indeed! Oh, it's outrageous! Mr. Thomas, how dare you!'' He took a couple of steps toward the defense table.

Bang . . . bang. Rile turned up his audio. "Will counsel approach the bench!"

"Gentlemen," said the chancellor sternly. "A couple of points. First: I will not permit these proceedings to turn into some crazy carnival. Holo and media coverage may continue in the mezzanine, but the courtroom here will be cleared. Second: Mr. Vulpin, you should be more considerate of your witness. You should have anticipated that Mr. Furkas could not endure the rigors of the witness chair. I'm going to discharge him now and strike all his testimony, direct and cross. Why are you smiling, Mr. Thomas?"

"Just happy the poor man will be spared further anguish, milord. I agree with you: Mr. Vulpin should get him to a doctor immediately. However, when—and if—he recovers, I may have some more questions."

Vulpin darted a dire and baleful look at his adversary, then helped a very puzzled man from the witness stand.

As he turned back to his table Thomas noted that the computer terminal was bringing in a message on the CRT. Dore was studying it carefully. Yes, it was from Wright back at PSI, and it was double-coded. The enemy—whoever they were—would of course eventually computer-break both codes, but it would take time, especially for Dore's secondary encryption. Thomas waited as his client finished decoding with his cranial implant, and then tuned quickly to Dore's mental transmission. The words took whispering form in his own cerebral chips.

TEN PERCENT PEACE COMMON OWNED BY KUDDER TEN BY VULPIN TEN BY BOSLOW SEVENTY BY PERSON UNIDENTIFIED.

Well, except for the mysterious rogue with seventy percent, there it was. He exchanged glances with Dore, who simply smiled his crooked smile.

"You called it correctly," whispered Thomas. "Legal murder."

Dore chuckled wryly. "And let the taxpayers pay for it. But don't lose heart, my young friend."

"Unless we do something drastic," warned Thomas, "that jury will convict you. Then he'll kill you—with your own guillotine, for God's sake."

"We're going to do something drastic," Dore assured him. "You'll see."

Thomas thought, Why do I trust this man? Twenty experts claim Jupiter can't blow. He says it will, and will do it before the day is done. I believe him. If he's insane, so am I.

The gavel again. "Gentlemen, it's a bit past twelve noon. Court will recess until one-thirty. As we adjourn, however, I'd like to see counsel in my chambers for a few minutes."

The reporter rose with his audiocorder. Rile waved him back down with a languid gesture. "We will not need you, Mr. Buchner. It will be off the record."

"I'll wait for you outside by the fountain," Dore told his lawyer. Thomas nodded.

"All rise," called the bailiff.

13
In Chambers

From the hag and hungry goblin
That into rags would rend ye,
And the spirit that stands by the naked man
In the book of Moons defend ye!
    —"Tom o' Bedlam"—(anonymous, 17th century)

Thomas and Vulpin followed the lord chancellor out through the back entrance to Rile's suite.

The instant he entered the room Thomas knew something was wrong. He identified the discontinuity instantly. A faint, tantalizing scent of flowers, perhaps no more than half a dozen molecules.

Nadys.

His eyes swept in swift probing jerks around the room. The only thing that might be considered unusual was a silver-coated plastic box on the chancellor's desk. Nothing else. She wasn't here. Then what—? How—?

He began to surmise, and to be afraid.

"Gentlemen," boomed the genial justice, "please be seated." He eased into the great plush chair behind the desk. "You there, if you please, Mr. Thomas."

The lawyer took the chair directly across the desk, facing Rile. Vulpin sat at the side.

The lord chancellor smiled. "You have done well so far, Mr. Thomas, very well indeed. Perhaps we underestimated you. Your cross of Mr. Furkas was a masterpiece. I'm sure Mr. Vulpin will want to bear in mind the proper technique for future operations. If any." He favored the people's prosecutor with an enigmatic stare. Vulpin lowered his eyes and seemed visibly to shrink.

"You did not call me here to congratulate me," said Thomas curtly. "What do you want?"

Rile pouted, then he sighed. "Oh very well. I'll come to the point." He leaned forward and stared hard and unblinking at the lawyer. "Give us Michael Dore. In return you can have the lady Nadys Blanding."

Vulpin added: "It's clean, efficient, sensible."

Quentin Thomas tried very hard to conceal his growing terror. Could they do this? Could these human rodents contrive the death of his beloved one-quarter million miles away?

Rile seemed to read his thoughts. He pursed his lips as if in sympathetic recognition of the lawyer's difficulty in dealing with this sudden onslaught of reality. He took the shimmering plastic box in both hands and pressed the edges. The lid sprang open.

Thomas caught the flood of odor instantly. His heart began to pound. Something of Nadys's was in that box. He stood and leaned over the desk.

Rile unwrapped golden tissue from around something filmy and iridescent. Lingerie—panties—carrying, where her hip would be, the letter "N." Rile held it up with thumbs and forefingers of both hands. He grinned happily at his victim. "This came in barely an hour ago, on the noon express. Do you recognize it, Mr. Thomas?"

He had taken it from her body on well-remembered occasions, but he would never let them know. Actually there had originally been four pieces—brassiere, panties, nightgown, and peignoir: his gift on her last birthday. All specially woven of chromo fiber so thin, so exquisite, that the four pieces together could be passed through that putative engagement ring. She could make them change color at will, through a combination of hormonal hints and cranial waves.

Even if these creatures could counterfeit the fabric—which he very much doubted—the odor was unique, and they probably did not know that only he could detect it.

He fought down a sense of desecration, violation . . . rape.

They were watching him, and he would not let them know anything.

It was not too difficult to figure out how they had stumbled onto her. This was the outcome of the camera on the hill outside Penal Systems, plus computer checks against her list of visitors.

"T—July 27," he said. " 'T' means terminate. You had planned to kill her this evening?" The gentleness in his voice amazed him. "She had assigned her meager assets over to you, and you were going to kill her routinely, as part of a systematic program. This trial, myself, Michael Dore, none of this had anything to do with T—July 27."

"Very perceptive, Mr. Thomas." Rile sounded sincerely regretful. "Yes, you're absolutely right. Actually, it begins tonight, when they're all in their beds. Less commotion that way. A little pill in her bedtime milk. Once the button is pushed, the computer gets to work, and from then on it's all automatic. The coroner's report, notification of the nearest relative or designated friend—you, I suppose, Mr. Thomas—and we hereby notify you—a fine, appreciative obituary for the papers, cremation, ashes in a gold-plated urn . . ." He eyed the lawyer speculatively. "But now you and Michael Dore and this trial are indeed closely connected to Ms. Nadys Blanding. Wouldn't you agree? And we're not going to let anything bad happen to her, are we, Mr. Thomas?"

"Nothing personal to any of you," said Vulpin brightly. "We assure you, it would have been quite routine. Ms. Blanding *did* assign all assets, in case of death while in residence."

Thomas said, "You want me to plead him guilty."

"Yes, I think so," said Rile. "As to the mechanics of the deal, I believe that would be the best way to approach it."

"He will of course disagree. There will be a scene in court."

"It doesn't matter. I will accept the change of plea, and so will the jury."

"A total betrayal of my client."

"Exactly," said Rile. "Do you have a problem with that?"

Thomas was silent. Just now he felt too stupid to say anything coherent or logical.

"Ms. Blanding lives, though," offered Vulpin cheerfully.

Thomas ignored him. "Dore dies," he said to Rile. "He dies by a change of plea. Or he dies if your remarkable jury brings him in guilty. Which they will. Either way, he dies. And certainly, you've got *her*. You don't need a guilty plea. Why are you doing this?"

"Insurance," said Vulpin.

"And think how it will look to the media," declared Rile. "His own lawyer giving up . . . admitting to six billion people that this man is a traitor to the human race."

"Betraying the betrayer?" said Thomas coolly

Rile chuckled "Oh, well said, Mr. Thomas. Really, sir, you should drop that poor fellow Dore, and come over to us."

"Or else?"

The lord chancellor laughed good-humoredly. "You certainly have a flair for succinct language, Mr. Thomas."

At this point several images flashed through the mind of Quentin Thomas. First was a vision of life without Nadys. He had a sensation of falling backward, over a cliff edge, down, down, down, into an abyss without bottom. It was dark, and dismal, and his eyes were rolling up into his head, and as he fell endlessly and forever, he pleaded with God Almighty (whose existence he had heretofore doubted) to let him die. The second image (he seemed to be going through images in the manner of the narrator in the Book of Revelation) was a clear visual scenario: If Rile killed Nadys, Rile couldn't afford to let him continue to live. Rile would also have to kill him. The alternative would be for him to kill Rile and Rile's incubus, the Honorable People's Prosecutor, Harry Vulpin. Since Rile controlled the Lunar Security Force, there could hardly be any doubt as to the outcome of *that* contest. And Dore, of course, was a predictable casualty in any case.

Logic required that he assent to the unthinkable. At least Nadys would live. Maybe.

On the other hand, he had never placed much faith in logic, and he deeply resented being told what he must do. He got to his feet. "I'll give you my answer in court."

"Meanwhile," said the lord chancellor, "please bear in mind that if you attempt to warn Ms. Blanding, directly or indirectly, through your Mr. Wright or otherwise, we will, shall we say, accelerate her program."

"So be smart," recommended Vulpin.

Thomas gave one last look at Nadys's intimacies. Rile caught the glance, seemed to think a moment, then wadded up the blithe garment like a handkerchief and held it to his face.

Don't do it, you bastard, Thomas warned mentally. He turned away as the lord chancellor blew his nose.

He could not look back. Strange, he thought, I don't feel murderous. Just . . . icy. Martin Rile has just committed suicide.

He left the chamber alone, passed down the side corridor, and out into the Rotunda.

And now what?

Tell Dore?

No.

If worst came to worst, would he take the deal? He'd rather die. But that was no answer at all.

He wished he had never heard of Penal Systems, Michael Dore, the moon.

Would Dore's idiotic psi-enhancer really work? More importantly, would it work for *him*? Siva had tried it and had lost his mind. Well, it *had* to work. It was that or destruction for all of them. It was his only chance to save Nadys . . . and Dore . . . and himself.

He hoped it would be a warm night in Howard County, Maryland.

The philanthropist was standing in front of the stock reporter screen just outside the Finance Wing.

Thomas walked over. "What's it doing?"

"Two and a quarter. Down a full point from this morning."

And it might well touch rock bottom before the evening is over, thought the lawyer. He ought to care, but somehow he couldn't. Not just now.

"What was on Rile's mind?" asked Dore.

The lawyer shook his head. "A tricky procedural question. But I think I can work it out, so let's set it aside for the moment. The big thing now is your psi-enhancer. It's in the base of the guillotine?"

Dore led him away from the fountain. "Yes, and we'll have to do something about the guard."

14
A Five-Letter Key

If the sun and moon should doubt
They'd immediately go out.
    —*William Blake, "Auguries of Innocence"*

Thomas looked over at the little group standing by the guillotine. Several were obviously just curious onlookers. One was a man in uniform, with sidearm and beeper. The lawyer said, "No problem. But how about the lock . . . a five-digit code?"

"Five letters."

"What's the code?"

Dore looked uncomfortable. "It's a random chaser."

Thomas gulped. "Totally random? And changes periodically?"

"Right."

"You'll have to guess what it is, at any given period?"

"Yes." Dore was apologetic. "I was thinking security, and I thought we'd have more time."

"How long is each five-letter solution on?"

"One second. It changes every second. It never repeats until it gets to the end of the random sequence. Then it starts over."

Thomas ran the numbers through his math microchip. 26^5 changes. 26^5 seconds. Then start over. 26^5 seconds equals . . . 137½ days. He would have to stand there for over nineteen weeks, hoping to impress the correct solution on the random selector as the letters flitted by. And if he didn't connect, then it's try again for another nineteen weeks.

It was at this moment that he understood the nature of

infinity, and how some infinities, though numerically smaller than others, are actually larger. The biggest practical number (he had read somewhere) was 10^{124}, which was the number of cubic fermis in the known universe. The number of atoms in the human body was supposed to be of the order of 8×10^{26}. Big numbers, both. But his particular infinity, 26^5, though numerically a fraction of these, was surely immensely greater in its registry on the human mind, because it was an infinity of time.

He groaned.

He couldn't stand here for nineteen weeks. Once he got rid of the guard, he estimated he'd have about five or six minutes to solve the key. Then the guard would discover the false alarm and would return running, probably with weapon drawn.

There had to be another way.

Rethink this thing. The random sequence was supposed to be nonrepeating, and it was supposed to use all five-letter combinations during a given run. After that the cycle would begin again. He would have to work within a given cycle. If he could hold *one* five-letter code on the lock while simultaneously speeding up the random spinner, he must inevitably force his solution on the lock. Solution and key would match, and the lock would open.

His cerebral cortex was making calculations and self-appraisals. That cortex contained, in its myriad intricate folds, some hundred billion neurons. Each "fired" a neural transmitter across a synapse of about 300–400 angstroms. There had to be a brief rest period of one-half to two milliseconds, say an average of one millisecond, before a given synapse could fire again. But that would mean a temporary loss of only one in every thousand cells. Not bad. During any given second, practically his entire mental organization could be available and working. The question was to break it down, give each of the five major cortical areas control over one of the five code letters—convert his brain into a network computer, as it were.

In effect, if he couldn't bring the correct key to the ever protean, ever changing code, he'd have to persuade that infinitely kaleidoscopic code to come to his invariant key. Eventually, they would have to match.

The next question was, could he force a segmented cortex to follow the whirling random codes, holding on to one five-letter key, until one of the codes matched his key? And what key could he hold in mental place until the code synchronized with it? Hah!

"Can you do it?" asked Dore uneasily.

"Maybe. Can the spinner take one hundred thousand changes a second?"

"I don't really know."

"Let's find out."

"First . . . the guard . . . ?"

"Right." Thomas was already analyzing the circuitry in the man's beeper. "There we go."

Be-e-ep . . . be-e-ep . . .

The guard fumbled a moment as he felt for the off button. The sound ceased. He held the unit to his ear. "Yes?" He tapped at it. "Jackson here. Hello? Hello?"

Be-e-ep . . . be-e-ep . . . be-e-ep . . .

Dore looked at Thomas in amazement.

"Emergency override," explained the lawyer. "He didn't even know he had it."

This time the guard made no effort to turn it off, but wheeled and dashed off to the Police Wing.

Even before the guard vanished, the two men were standing by the guillotine.

Thomas sensed inward, through the panel walls, and found the random spinner. Curious, this little piece of electronic wizardry controlled not only the panel lock; it also served the three cables that would launch the guillotine blade in lethal flight. But no time to think about that. He listened to the spinner a moment. Click . . . click . . . One a second. He increased the speed. Clickclickclick . . . It began to hum in his mind, then reached twenty thousand cycles per second, the upper limit of the human audible range . . . then leaped into ultrasound. He let it rise to what he estimated was one hundred thousand random sets per second. He held it there. Simultaneously he concentrated on the one set he knew he could hold in his mind unwavering forever: NA-DYS.

Within seconds the hinged lid flipped back.

Dore reached in and pulled out something. A black box—about the size, shape, and texture of a legal briefcase. His client snapped the panel door in place. "Come on. Let's get back to A-A."

"Later," interjected Thomas. "Just now I have to use it for something personal."

"Personal? I don't understand." Dore's brow furrowed deeply.

The lawyer realized he'd have to tell him. "It's Nadys, my lady, back at Patuxent Haven. They are threatening to kill her."

"Oh God!" Dore was silent a moment. Then he said, "A tradeoff? Me for her? That's what that little chambers conference was all about?"

"Yes."

"What did you tell them?"

"I said I'd give them an answer this afternoon in court."

"Well. I see. I assure you, Quentin, I didn't know it would come to this. I guess we'd better get to work immediately. But we can't work here."

"All right. Back to A-A, then. We'll take a cart. You can explain the mechanism on the way."

They climbed into the nearest autocart. Thomas took a moment to check the circuitry. It was clean. He dropped a coin in the slot, punched in "A-A", and off they went.

"It's really quite simple," explained Dore. From the box he pulled out two antennae and a filament plug-in, which he handed to Thomas. "This should fit your cranial socket."

"Then what?"

"You *will* yourself to be there."

"Two hundred and forty thousand miles away?"

"You can do it."

Siva couldn't, mused Thomas. No matter. *He* could. He had to.

The lawyer took the plug and stuck it into his ear socket. The click was the last sensory input from life on Luna for long long moments.

There was an interval of darkness and bitter cold.

When his head cleared he was in the lobby of Patuxent Haven. Not all of him, of course: just that part of him that could control the world of subparticles. But it was sufficient.

Where now? Should he look for Nadys? No. No time.

Down this corridor. The locked medical dispensary. That's where all the death-dealing pills were kept. He short-circuited the lights, the drug-metering systems, the heating systems, the microwave autoclaves. He activated all fire alarms and all water sprinklers throughout all the halls, dormitory rooms, service rooms, rec room, offices, and auditorium. He then stood by for a moment, waiting until he could sense guests milling about and being directed out onto the broad lawns. Nadys would certainly be among them. Very satisfactory. Fire fighters from all over the country would be responding within minutes. You're safe for tonight, my naiad Nadys, he thought, along with perhaps several other of your friends pre-marked "T—July 27."

And that's just the curtain-raiser. Let's get down to business.

Where's the central data bank?

Wow! Pay dirt! Right here in Howard County, the comprehensive data banks for all Peace Eternal homes all over the world! Millions of names. How to do this? They have an auto-erase. Start with Blanding, Nadys. After that, just a question of keeping it on automatic, no-override, until the end. That should do it.

And now it's time to get back to Luna.

Tell Rile that I have upset his deadly little applecart? Certainly not. No call to alarm the dear chap. Play it cool. Very cool. Am I still angry? I don't really know. Am I still going to kill him? No. That would be, as he says, uncouth. I'm going to let him do it himself. And so Thomas was thinking as his mind cleared.

He was still in the autocart, and it was now standing just outside the A-A. Dore was sitting there beside him, watching him with a blend of anxiety and relief.

"Are you all right?" asked his client.

"I'm fine."

"Did it work?"

"I think so."

"What did you do?"

"Theoretically, I wrecked the place."

"That ought to take their minds off her." Dore was thoughtful. "Do you think we should ask Henry Wright to verify?"

"No. They are monitoring all message traffic, and just to ask the question would tell them something. Actually, I think there's a better and quicker way."

"Which is?"

"If it worked, Rile's clerk is going to bring him a note. A very disconcerting note. Within an hour or two. I expect we'll be in court at the time, and we'll know as soon as Rile knows."

"Fair enough. We wait. So, shall we go on upstairs?"

15
Under Hydrogen Seas

Soon as the evening shades prevail,
The moon takes up the wondrous tale.
  —Joseph Addison, "Ode"

Thomas unplugged the enhancer and returned it to Dore. They got out of the cart and proceeded with studied insouciance on up the steps into the inn, where they picked up carry-out sandwiches at the lunch bar. And thence up the escalator to Room 41.

"We still have two problems," said Dore. "Number one, blowing Jupiter. Number two, proving we did it. How can we show off our nice new sun to a skeptic court and jury?"

"I have an idea," said Thomas. "Jarvis of the Geologic Survey is on this afternoon, right?"

"Theoretically."

"And he can pinpoint his upcoming nuclear shot on a good map?"

"Again, theoretically."

"Now, let's think architecturally a moment."

"Proceed, counselor."

"Yesterday evening I was walking around in the Rotunda, and I took a good look at the dome."

"So?"

"The dome has a precisely defined focus and directrix, which means it's a perfect parabola."

"I'll take your word for it."

"Now, let's switch to the here and now." Thomas reached over and picked up a wine goblet from a serving tray and examined it critically. "Exquisite workmanship.

Venetian? Very thin. Diameter at focus, about three point three centimeters, wouldn't you say? And precisely parabolic. They're the best, though sphericals and ellipsoids will work, too.''

"The best for *what*?" asked Dore curiously.

Thomas tied a string to the goblet stem. "Here, hold this. Over the wastebasket." He picked up the keyboard. "How high does this go?"

"Maximum frequency is about twelve thousand."

"Good enough. We'll need about ten thousand. Now then, you were going to give me a recital, but we'll turn it around. *I'll* give *you* one." He began on the keyboard, starting in the lower registers, going up key by key, shriller, and finally screeching.

Crack!

Dore held the stem by the attached string. The rest had fallen into the wastebasket.

"There," said Thomas.

The philanthropist shrugged unhappily as he dropped the residue into the basket. "There, *what*?"

Thomas unreeled the communicator filament from his ear insert and handed it to Dore, who duly plugged it into his own cranial socket. Ultra-secret. He nodded to the lawyer.

"The wavelength of the final sound was three point three centimeters, the same as the glass. The Rotunda dome is ten meters in diameter. Moonquake waves are about ten meters long. We are going to make a nice moonquake that will blow the dome. Whereupon his lordship can step outside his door and look straight up at the sky.''

"And just where are you going to find a ten-meter moonquake?"

"We don't think we should hold up Dr. Jarvis's seismic shot any longer."

"Ah! Of *course*!"

"But we'll have to schedule everything very carefully," warned Thomas. "You say Jupiter reaches zenith at exactly five this afternoon? The dome will have to blow no later than that, and, if we can, we should probably delay to the exact moment. Can we do that?"

"I foresee no difficulty. However, we bear in mind it

will take about two hours for Jupe to expand to full size, but it takes only about seven minutes for our nice little moonquake to reach here. So you'll have to do your big stunt with Jupe well before you blow Jarvis's little nuke."

"You're right. In that case, we'd better start with Jupiter, right now." He took the little black box from the philanthropist, pulled out the antennae and earplug. And now he found himself wondering. He had made it work in Patuxent Haven, but Jupiter was many times farther away than Earth. "Mike," he muttered, "can it really work at such a distance?"

The other laughed. "You're asking *me*? You're now the expert. *You* tell me. You have to believe in an occasional miracle, son. You have to believe that sometimes the good guys win. Yes, it'll work. You made it work once, and you can do it again. I don't think the greater distance will really be much of a factor. But just in case, why don't we find out?"

The lawyer did not know whether to laugh or shiver. Shiver? Siva? Poor choice of words, he thought.

"You can do it," insisted Dore. "You have tremendous psi—of exactly the right kind. You've already shown that. On Jupiter, of course, you'll be working with nuclear particles, not the electrical circuitry you were controlling back at the Haven. But it's all much the same. The geography is a little different, to be sure, but it ought not be a problem. Just now Jupiter is about six hundred million kilometers away. But with the enhancer you can vector out through the dimensions and hook on to the planet as though it were Patuxent Haven. You'll get there, and when you do, you must search out the Great Red Spot. You follow it down, through the gases—mostly hydrogen and helium—down, on down, to the metallic hydrogen shell. You don't stop there. You keep going. The nuclear waste will have sunk to the very inmost rocky core—where the heavy stuff collects. Our pile is probably all crumpled up into a raggedy pancake the size of metropolitan New York, sandwiched in between the liquid hydrogen shell and the rocky core."

"A needle in a haystack."

"Yes and no. It's showering radioactive particles all over

the place. You'll sense it right away. Look for uranium and plutonium. There's plenty there, a lot more than you'll need. Collect a stream of neutrons. Focus them at a cluster of uranium atoms. At that pressure you'll reach critical mass almost instantly. You'll get fission, and a high local temperature, at least one million Celsius. Also, there's lots of deuterium there—heavy hydrogen—concentrated by the high gravity. And in that high temperature zone, you'll be bringing a proton and a deuterium together. They'll fuse, and you'll get tritium. And now you're off and running. Two tritiums fuse to give helium 4 plus two protons and loads of energy, and you start over again. It'll happen just the way Zole explained. He's been a big help. Poor devil, won't he be surprised.''

And maybe so will I, thought Thomas. He said, ''Will I be able to sense the approach of critical mass? Will I be able to get out?''

''The safety factor is—adequate.''

''Translation: I could be killed.''

Dore sighed. ''You could.''

''Can *you* do it, Mike?''

''No. I've tried. I have some psi, but not enough of the right kind.'' He studied the lawyer somberly. ''Are you afraid?''

Thomas didn't answer. He fought down an urge to tell this strange man to go to hell, and then to run from the room, take a cart down to spaceport, and never see Dore again. Why didn't he do this? Nadys was now safe. She wasn't a factor. Maybe because he had taken the case, and now he had to see it through. Not to mention that his life was at risk, and that he would probably not get off the moon alive until he had settled with the lord chancellor. So he had to try to ignite Jupiter, even if it killed him. Which indeed it might.

Dore said quietly, ''You don't have to do it. I hereby relieve you.''

''If I don't do it, you'll be guillotined.''

''I suppose that's a possibility,'' agreed Dore.

''Actually,'' mused the lawyer, ''I have been wondering whether I could do it. Well, all right then, let's get started.

If I don't come back, tell my partners in Washington so they can bury me properly.''

Did Dore smile at that? He didn't know and didn't care.

Thomas plugged the cranial cable into his temporal insert and flipped the toggle switch. He blacked out instantly and began moving. He knew he was moving over a great distance; yet he had no sense of real motion. He seemed to be in many places at once.

He searched in the bitter cold blackness, and he found what he wanted. Past moonlets and hints of planetary rings. And then the swirling orange and pink bands, and there, finally, the GRS, big enough to swallow Earth at a gulp. And down and down, in the incredible whirling tube, thousands upon thousands of kilometers. And still down, ever through immense depths of hydrogen gas.

Finally he sensed a jar. Nothing solid. Just slower going. He was moving through liquid metallic hydrogen, heavily laced with deuterium. Then another jar. His mind was now resting on a great platform of crushed metal, surrounded by a cyclonic soup of radioactive particles. A decade of nuclear waste, just sitting there, waiting for him.

Ah, a goodly clump of U-235 atoms. All nicely oscillating. Start with just one. Just a question of hitting it with a neutron when it reaches that certain dumbbell configuration. Bang! Gotcha! It breaks up instantly into barium 141 and krypton 92, plus three new neutrons. And now we're in business. Everything goes. Every atom heavier than bismuth is unstable. Hey, this is *fun*! He didn't have to stir up any more neutrons, but out of a sense of total exhilaration, he did. He blew his mind through a few layers of plutonium 239. The neutrons spun out like frightened sparrows, then settled into illusory safety in neighboring atoms—which began breaking up. And more neutrons . . . many many more . . . critical mass was on the way, and when it came, fission would be total: one hundred percent. And the local temperature would jump to one million and it would keep climbing. And then hydrogen would begin to fuse with deuterium, which would then make tritium, then helium, and a lot more heat. The great metallic hydrogen core would become a giant fusion bomb. Jupiter would blow. And all this in nanoseconds. God! He had to get out! Quickly!

Up . . . cold gases . . . cold space . . . but it has been too much. He should have turned off . . . Had he gone past his exit? Now he can't return. He can't get back into his head. Is this death? Is he dead? No, he doesn't really believe he's dead. But where is he? Is he *any*where? Is this what happened to Siva?

Nadys! he shrieked. Help me! Where are you?

And there she stood. No, it's Dore, whacking at his face with a wet towel. Wham! Slam! "Quentin! Wake up! Hey, Quent!" Slap! Smack! "Ah, there you are! Are you all right? Quentin?"

"Yes, I think so . . ."

The other peered down eagerly at the white face. "Did you start the fission?"

"Fission? Oh, well, maybe. And maybe beyond that. Fusion. I think."

"What do you mean, you *think*? Did you, or didn't you?"

"Mike, no way to be absolutely sure. Not just yet."

"No, I guess not. But if you *were* sure, maybe we could just ignore the trial—not go back into court?"

"Too risky, Mike. Even if we were certain, you'd still have to go back. Otherwise Rile would send the police after you. Vulpin would call it flight from prosecution and a confession of guilt. Your bail would be forfeited. The jury would vote immediately. You'd be strapped into your guillotine before two o'clock."

"I see your point. All right, let's play it by the book. But assuming your ignition was successful, how long do you think it'll take to show something?"

"It should be evident by your five o'clock deadline." He unplugged the cable, pushed the antennae back in to their slots, and closed up the box. "Here's how we'll do it. This afternoon Vulpin will put on Jarvis and Boslow. You know Jarvis—the director of the Lunar Geological Survey. And of course Boslow. Boslow will give a deposition, live from Io. Both will testify as nuclear experts, to the effect that Jupiter cannot ignite."

"Interesting," said Dore. "If I have calculated the mathematics correctly, and if Boslow comes on after Jarvis, we may be able to watch the initial phases of the ignition by holo right in the courtroom.'' He glanced over at the wall clock. ''And I see our lunch hour is about over.'' He picked up the psi-enhancer. ''Let's go.''

16
While Back on Io

What is crooked cannot be made straight.
   —*Ecclesiastes 1:15*

Court convened.

His lordship looked down at Thomas speculatively. He rumbled, "Does either counsel have a motion at this time?"

Vulpin glanced covertly over at Thomas.

Rile seemed to sigh. "Mr. Vulpin?"

"Nothing at this time, milord."

"Mr. Thomas?" The chancellor leaned forward slightly.

Defense counsel answered coldly, "Nothing just now, milord." He noticed from the corner of his eye that his client was smiling faintly. But suppose the enhancer hadn't worked to destroy Patuxent Haven? Suppose Dore one day asked him, would you have pleaded me guilty then? Thomas never wanted that question put to him.

His lordship shrugged, leaned back, and signaled to Vulpin to call his next witness.

The prosecutor rose. "Next, milord, gentlemen of the jury, the people will interview Mr. William Boslow, manager of Arthur Clarke Station on Io, one of the larger moons of Jupiter. The interview will be live, by closed circuit holo. We—"

"Objection, milord," said Thomas. "This proposed interview violates the basic rules of evidence. Mr. Boslow will be responding to the learned prosecutor's preprinted interrogatory. That's easy enough for Mr. Vulpin's direct. But Jupiter and Io are over forty minutes away by electromagnetic transmission. Forty-five there, forty-five back: an hour and a half per question. A proper cross-examination will be impossible.''

The chancellor motioned both lawyers up to the bench. ''Mr. Vulpin?'' he queried.

''Cross-examination is not required in all cases, milord. I offer the Boslow interview as an exhibit, equivalent to a scientific treatise, admissible by judicial notice.''

''Interesting theory.'' Rile rubbed his chin. ''Well, why not? I'll let it in, and the jury can deal with it. They don't have to believe a word of it.''

''There's another problem,'' said Thomas. ''Mr. Boslow ought to be evacuated from Io Station immediately.''

Vulpin laughed. ''We address that problem in the interview.''

''So, go ahead, Mr. Vulpin,'' said the lord chancellor.

''I'm afraid we've lost the first few minutes,'' said the prosecutor. ''While we have been arguing, Mr. Boslow has been broadcasting. But it's all recorded, and we can go back later to his opening remarks.''

The great wall holo stage sprang to life.

''Waste comes into this chute,'' a voice was explaining. (Thomas assumed it was Boslow, the station engineer.) ''It has to be repacked in canisters—actually a roomy little rocket. We can aim the rocket by adjusting the gantry angle. However, the best procedure is to wait for the GRS to approach from the left, then fire directly overhead, like leading a flying duck. Just take the readings and punch everything into the computer!

''We'll leave the docks now, and we'll take the rim corridor on our way back to the central instrument room, the scenic route, as it were. Gives you a nice view through the portholes. We'll pause here a moment.

''As you can see, the station sits on the rim top of a crater—the John Kennedy—and from here, through the ports you can get a fair view of the Ionian lowlands.

''Io's claim to fame of course is her volcanoes. There's one over there to the west. You can just barely make it out on the horizon, quiet just now, but last month we had an impressive three-day blast of sulfur dioxide. So far as we know Io and Terra have the only active volcanoes in the solar system. Aside from the volcanoes, not much to see, actually. The rest is like Luna: craters, maria, rubble, breccia. Dramatic bright and dark contrasts. Let's go on.

"We've seen the incoming waste dock, the exit rocket dock, the dormitory, the kitchen, recreation room, and that about completes the tour of the station. We're now back in the Central Control Room." The speaker smiled and sat down at a gauge-filled panel. "Everything means something, of course. Air pressure. Water pressure. Roentgen indices for receiving and discharge docks." He reached over and tapped a couple of the dials. "They can't really get stuck, but of course it's a good idea to make sure. These measure Jupiter's temperature, both at the surface and at the core. Surface is normally minus one hundred thirty degrees Celsius. Core temperature is something of a guess, of course, because we can sense it only indirectly. We give it a nominal thirty thousand. You have to go through over sixty-two thousand kilometers of hydrogen to get to the rocky core. Theoretically we have a pile of nuclear waste sitting at that hydrogen/silicate interface. But for all the good it's doing, it might as well be on Betelgeuse." He grinned engagingly at his unseen audience. "Anyhow, readings are recorded automatically. Over the past three years the greatest variations have been in the five- to ten-degree range, and we account for these by big surface storms that churn up gas layers right down to the metallic hydrogen shell.

"These green lights show that everything is cool"—he grinned archly into the camera—"at the Jovian core. A mere thirty thousand degrees. If the core starts to warm up beyond that, the lights turn red and begin to flash. I understand bells will start ringing all over the station." More smiles. "There's absolutely no danger. Jupiter is not going to ignite during my lifetime.

"Now then, let me get to this interrogatory." He unfolded the papers and adjusted his spectacles. "Question number one. Do I anticipate any major temperature changes in Jupiter in the near future? The answer is no.

"Question number two. Will Jupiter ignite by seventeen hundred, July 27, Lunar Time? Well, I pretty much answered that already, didn't I? No, Jupiter is not going to ignite by July 27. Sorry, Lamplighters.

"Question number three: Dr. Boslow, are are you aware that you and Arthur Clarke Station will be consumed utterly if Jupiter ignites July 27? Yes, I am well aware of that. But I'm not worried. It isn't going to ignite.

"Question number four. Where is Jupiter just now, with respect to the station? On the dark side of Io. That's why you don't see it when you look out the side ports. But we'll soon be in the light side; here comes the terminator. And I should mention an oddity here. Io revolves every forty-two plus hours, whereas Jupiter revolves every nine plus hours. That means Jupiter revolves four and one-third times while we are revolving once. We see the whole planet, Red Spot and all, several times per Ionian day.

"Question number five. Can you leave your camera focussed on your temperature gauges and alarm lights for the next several hours, and at least until five o'clock? Sure, no problem." He pointed. "That's the main gauge, remember? We'll just keep an eye on it. If Jupiter ignites, red lights will start flashing here and all over the station, and you'll hear bells clanging. That's not going to happen, you understand, but at least that's what the emergency circuitry provides for." He faced the cameras again in a gesture of simple flowing sincerity. "I would like to emphasize one thing. Even though the Lamplighter Project can't ignite this planet, the program is not totally useless. We are indeed disposing of terrestrial nuclear waste. Whereas we used to shoot it into the sun, we now drop it into the GRS. A bit more expensive, perhaps, since just now we have to fight solar gravity, but useful nevertheless."

Damned with faint praise, thought Thomas. The kiss of death, the *coup de grâce*.

His lordship gave the lawyer a long speculative look. The gaze seemed to be a mix of questions, accusations, and threats. He's wondering, thought counsel for the defense, whether I have agreed to his deal, and if so, when I'm going to abandon Michael Dore. Well, let him wonder. He'll soon get news from Maryland. Then let him *really* wonder.

Meanwhile we'll go on with the farce . . . silly courtroom

chatter . . . question . . . answer . . . objection . . . sustained . . . overruled . . . riposte . . . parry. It's all a smokescreen to hide the real battle. I have to win that battle or die. Rile can't let either of us leave the moon alive. Well, we'll see about that. Counsel for the defense and his strange client have resources that milord chancellor and his cohorts cannot possibly imagine. Actually, mused Thomas, the opposing combatants stand in fair balance. The next couple of hours would decide everything.

17
Like a Bell

Let there be light.
  —Genesis 1:3

And so to the next witness.

"Dr. Jarvis," asked Vulpin, "what is your educational background and professional experience?"

"Ph.D. in nuclear physics, Chicago Institute, then five years Federation Nuclear Commission; presently director, Lunar Geologic Survey."

"Have you published any papers in the nuclear field?"

"About sixty; several still in the hands of the editors."

"Are you familiar with the Lamplighter Project?"

"Just the nuclear side."

"Explain, please."

"I have followed all the material published by the Lamplighters, and I have made periodic appraisals of the project."

"Why? For whom?"

"For various governments and other organizations who have contributed money to the project."

"They wanted to know whether they were throwing money down a rat hole?"

Thomas jumped up. "Objection!"

"Overruled," said Rile. "The language is a bit colorful, but the meaning is clear and acceptable."

Thomas was about to say something further, but Dore tugged at his sleeve. He sat down.

Thus encouraged, Vulpin continued. "And *were* they?"

"Were they what?"

"Throwing their money down a rat hole?"

"Well, that depends."

(An honest man? thought Thomas. What's he doing here?)

"Depends on what?" said the prosecutor.

"Time . . . patience . . . money . . . enough nuclear material. If nuclear waste is shot into the planet at the present rate for another three hundred years it will almost certainly ignite."

"Three hundred years?"

"Actually, three hundred and two, plus or minus ninety days."

"Are you aware, Dr. Jarvis, that Mr. Dore has promised to ignite Jupiter by an hour not later than five o'clock this afternoon?"

"I believe I read that in the Lamplighter prospectus."

(Here comes the hypothetical, thought Thomas.)

Vulpin said, "In your professional opinion as a nuclear physicist, is it possible for the planet Jupiter to ignite today?"

"No, sir."

"Tomorrow?"

"No, sir. It's like I said, Mr. Vulpin. It would take at least three hundred years."

"Thank you, doctor." Vulpin turned to face the wall screen. "Oh . . . and if court and counsel will indulge a factual statement for the record, let us take note that the Io Station has changed not one iota since Dr. Boslow's testimony."

They all looked over at the big wall holo panel. No action there.

"So noted, Mr. Vulpin," rumbled Rile. "Please get on with it."

"Nothing further, milord." Vulpin bestowed his most winning smile on Thomas. "Truth drug, Mr. Thomas?"

"Waived."

"Your witness, then."

"Thank you." Counsel for the defense smiled back as he passed between the tables and approached the witness box. "Dr. Jarvis, you mentioned that you are presently director of the Lunar Geologic Survey?"

"Yes, sir."

"You have offices right here in the Rotunda complex?"

"Yes sir, right off the Rotunda."

"And you have an exhibit just inside your lobby?"

"Yes, sir. A model of a proposed seismic shot."

"Tell us about the shot, Dr. Jarvis."

Vulpin objected from his seat. "This is all irrelevant. Move to strike all cross so far."

"Dr. Jarvis," said Thomas smoothly, "would you please explain to the court the relevance of your proposed seismic shot?"

"It's a nuclear shot."

Vulpin looked doubtful. "I still don't see—"

The chancellor glowered down at Thomas. "Does this bear on the witness's qualification as a nuclear expert?"

"Yes, milord."

"You should have objected before the hypothetical. But let it go."

"Thank you, milord." (Ah, if you only knew!) "Now, Dr. Jarvis, would you please describe your proposed seismic shot. What's the purpose?"

"I thought that was pretty well known."

"For the record, please, doctor."

"Well, we use conventional seismic techniques. The bomb is buried in a five-hundred-meter shaft drilled in solid basalt. We'll explode it, and the explosion will generate seismic waves. The waves will pass through all kinds of lunar features. We're looking especially for water, or more specifically, minerals that contain water of crystallization. These are all silicates of aluminum with alkali and alkaline earth metals. There are over sixty, and some of the deposits are believed to be quite extensive. The shock waves will hit these deposits and pass on to dozens of seismometers placed at strategic points around the moon. There they are recorded and computer analyzed. The wave forms as received will identify the mineral, quantity, location, depth, and so on."

"And suppose, Dr. Jarvis, you locate a suitable water-bearing mineral, how would you get the water out?''

''Probably by the Frasch process—we'd sink a superheated steam line into the formation, volatilize the water, then condense it near the surface. It's conceivable, of course, that the shock itself could dissociate H_2O from the mineral, and we could get an artesian flow.''

''All this is basically just a lunar adaptation of a terran technique?''

''Very similar.''

''Will these lunar waves be felt here?''

''Yes, but only by our seismometers. Not by people. The chandeliers won't sway. The dishes won't rattle. Nobody in Lunaplex will know, unless he's watching a seismometer.''

''Too weak, doctor?''

''Far too weak. The bomb's on the other side of the moon. At the antipodes, as a matter of fact.''

''The antipodes? Where would that be, doctor?''

''It's in the middle of a triangle bounded by three well known craters: Jules Verne, Gagarin, and Tsiolkovskii.''

''How far away is that?''

''Depends on how you measure the distance. Waves coming through the lunar center—P waves—will of course travel one lunar diameter, about 3,460 kilometers. Waves moving on the surface—S waves—travel a full lunar semicircle: about 5,435 kilometers.''

''P waves are faster and would arrive here first?'' asked Thomas.

''Yes, P first, then S. Actually, both would be expected to continue for several minutes, and there might be some overlap.''

''But neither would be detectable by normal human senses? Here, I mean.''

''No, just by our instruments.''

''But you're shooting a nuclear bomb?''

''Yes, sir.''

''And it'll make a pretty big bang?''

''So-so. About like the little ones at Hiroshima and Nagasaki.''

''What if I told you, doctor, that your little bomb packs

enough power to bring down the great dome?''

The savant took that one calmly. ''I'd say you're crazy, or ill-informed, or both.''

Thomas smiled. ''You know how the Apollo astronauts described the way the moon reacted to a meteor impact?''

''Yes. They said it rang like a bell.''

''But you don't think it's going to ring like a bell?''

''Not this far away from epicenter.''

''Let's get back to moonquake waves, doctor. You mentioned P waves. Pressure waves, I think you called them. How fast do they travel? Begin with your explosion at five hundred meters depth.''

''Well, we start with movement through the crust. P velocity is slow at first: two to four kilometers per second, but getting faster all the time as we go deeper. We hit a discontinuity at about twenty-five kilometers, where wave speed increases to about five kilometers, then another increase to about six kilometers. At sixty kilometers depth we leave the crust and enter the mantle, and we get another immediate increase, to about eight kilometers per second, which increases further to about nine kilometers per second down to a depth of about nine hundred kilometers. There we leave the mantle, enter the asthenosphere, and then into the molten iron core—some seven hundred kilometers diameter. Here our values become a bit hazy, but in random shots into and through the core we have encountered velocities as high as nine point two kilometers per second and as low as seven kilometers per second.''

''All in all, what would you estimate as the average velocity of a P wave leaving your explosion site and coming straight here?''

''About eight kilometers per second.''

''So, in seconds, we're talking a travel time of 3,460 divided by eight?''

''Yes. That would be about four hundred and thirty seconds, or about seven minutes.''

''That's pretty fast, isn't it, doctor?''

''It's all relative. It's several times faster than the speed of sound, but of course nowhere near the speed of light.

Eniwetok Atoll to the California coast took just a little longer: twelve minutes.''

''Now, doctor, let's turn our attention to the bomb itself. Would you please describe it.''

''Certainly. Actually, it's pretty well known. We have issued a press release—'' He pulled a paper from a jacket pocket.

''We can take that in evidence later, if need be,'' said Thomas. ''Meanwhile, perhaps you could provide a good layman's description, for the benefit of the court, in your own words. For example, how big is it?''

''I see what you mean. All right, it's about the size of a grapefruit, with a plutonium core, covered with a beryllium neutron reflector about one centimeter thick. The reflector is coated with C-4, which is a mixture of TNT and a plasticizer. It's a good neutron reflector as well as the starting explosive. A fuse—an electrical detonator—is imbedded in the C-4. The fuse blows the C-4, and when the compression wave hits the center of the plutonium, it goes supercritical. That's about it.'' He looked down questioningly at Thomas.

''What yield, doctor?''

''About fourteen percent.''

''Isn't that pretty low?''

''No, actually it's average. State of the art. And it's just as well.''

''Why is that?''

''If it were much higher—say twenty percent, we'd feel tremors here.''

''How about fifty percent yield?''

''Well, assuming a focus here at Lunaplex, I expect it would rattle the dome.''

''But you see no danger?''

''Absolutely none.''

''Is the bomb connected up and ready to blow?''

''No.''

''It can't possibly go off by accident?''

''No. The ignition circuitry has yet to be installed. That will take several days. We don't want to start just yet.''

''Why the delay?''

"We're waiting for this trial to finish." The scientist looked uncomfortable.

Can't fault him for watching out for the annual appropriation, thought Thomas. But no harm getting in a little dig. "You mean all the cameras and media men are occupied right now."

"Ob—"began Vulpin.

Thomas grinned. "Strike that. Is it your testimony, doctor, that your little grapefruit-size bomb cannot be exploded without its auxiliary electric assemblies?"

"Quite so."

"You've heard of psi fusion, doctor?"

The witness shrugged. "Yes."

"You don't believe in it?"

"No, of course not."

"You don't think psi could explode your bomb and blow the great dome?"

"Really, Mr. Thomas!"

"I take that to mean no. Well, then, Dr. Jarvis, if at a specific point in time I tell you that your bomb has blown with a ninety-five plus percent yield, and seven minutes later the great dome shatters, would you accept that as evidence that psi can detonate nuclear material?"

Dr. Jarvis turned to face Rile. "Milord, with all due respect to the judicial system, this man is insane."

The lord chancellor gave him a comfortable smile. "Personally, I think you're right, doctor. And as soon as this trial is over, we'll try to do something about it. Meanwhile, however, would you please answer the question."

"Very well. If you put it that way, Mr. Thomas, just as a hypothetical, I suppose that would be evidence that psi can detonate nuclear material. Actually, though, psi can't detonate *anything*."

Thomas pressed on. "And if that should happen, would you acknowledge certain fundamental gaps in your nuclear expertise?"

"I suppose. So go ahead, psi my bomb, Mr. Thomas."

"I intend to, Dr. Jarvis. But all in good time. We'd like your bomb to coincide with the ignition of Jupiter, which should be directly overhead about five o'clock. As you can see from Dr. Boslow's temperature dials''—he waved at the wall holo—''nothing seems to be happening on Jupiter just yet. But it's coming.''

They all turned to look at the holo screen.

Jarvis laughed and shook his head.

Thomas smiled and nodded to Vulpin. ''Nothing further.''

18
Grapefruit and Dome

To pluck bright honor from the pale-faced moon.
  —William Shakespeare, King Henry IV, Part I

"No redirect," said the prosecutor. "That's the case for the people."

"Thank you, Mr. Vulpin," said the chancellor. "Mr. Thomas, do you wish to offer a motion at this time?"

"Why yes, milord, I do indeed wish to offer a motion."

Rile exhaled heavily and leaned forward expectantly. Vulpin flashed a hard victorious grin at the visiting lawyer. Michael Dore looked up in sudden dismay. "Relax," Thomas hissed at him from the corner of his mouth. "I'm not about to plead you guilty. We just need to drag it out a little."

The lord chancellor called out, "Proceed, Mr. Thomas. What is your motion?"

"I move to dismiss all counts as not proven beyond a reasonable doubt," said Thomas blandly. "The testimony of the three so-called technical experts to the effect that Jupiter cannot be ignited by five this afternoon is meaningless for the simple reason that it isn't five o'clock yet. On the other hand, if they want to come back after five and testify again, that would likewise be meaningless and useless, because by then we would know one way or the other whether Jupiter is a second sun. And of course the testimony of Mr. Furkas simply shows that powerful forces are trying to frame the defendant. When—"

Vulpin was on his feet, outraged. "Objection! All testimony by poor Mr. Furkas was stricken. There was no testimony left to show anything.''

The lord chancellor banged his gavel. "We can save time here, Mr. Thomas. The sense of your motion is, insufficient evidence to go to the jury. I rule that there is sufficient evidence, and your motion is therefore denied.'' His voice was cold and grim. "That brings us to the next question. Are you putting on a case?''

"I am indeed, your honor.''

"Call your first witness.''

"I call Michael Dore.''

The defendant was duly sworn in, and he took the stand.

"Milord,'' said Thomas, "before we proceed, I will ask the clerk to mark for identification a certain device, namely this black box, some twenty by twenty by fifteen centimeters, weighing about ten kilos.''

The clerk stuck a label on the box. "That'll be your D-1, for identification.'' He handed it to the bailiff, who took it up to the bench. The lord chancellor looked at it dubiously. Vulpin walked up and also examined it.

"Just how is this thing relevant to these proceedings?'' demanded Rile.

"In two ways, milord. First, it's relevant to the ignition of Jupiter. Second, it's relevant in that it will make the ignited Jupiter visible to this court. Your lordship will recall that both objects, if achieved, will require taking the verdict from the jury and dismissal of the case. If I can refresh your lordship's memory by direct reference to the transcript—''

"Don't play games with me, Mr. Thomas. All right, go ahead, ignite Jupiter, and let us all take a look. And let me refresh *your* recollection: You do it by seventeen hundred hours—five o'clock.''

"Of course, milord. Actually, we've already started. Using this device, we initiated the ignition of Jupiter during the lunch recess.''

The chancellor looked skeptically toward the wall holo screen. "I don't see any change.''

"No, your honor. There's an induction period—a modest lag time. There has to be a fair amount of deuterium fusion before the temperature rise begins to show on Dr. Boslow's gauges, and then of course there's another forty-five minutes for the scene to be transmitted here. All in all, we should have strong evidence of ignition by five P.M. So with your lordship's permission, I shall now use this psi device to provide a good view of the new sun.''

Vulpin just shook his head. ''You're moonstruck, Thomas. Class A claustro.''

The court reporter looked up at the prosecutor. Her mouth framed the question, ''On the record?''

''Yeah,'' said Vulpin. ''On the record. He's crazy. If that's libel, let him sue me.''

The chancellor frowned at Vulpin and cleared his throat. ''How does it work?'' he asked Thomas.

''With your lordship's permission,'' said Thomas smoothly, ''Mr. Dore will provide details from the stand. Are there any objections to the exhibit? Mr. Vulpin?''

''No objection'' Vulpin added dryly, ''And I can hardly wait to see it ignite Jupiter.''

''It already has,'' said Thomas patiently. ''I explained that.''

''Let's get on with it,'' grumbled Rile. He glanced up at the clock. ''It's now sixteen thirty-five. Mr. Dore literally breaks his contract at five P.M., seventeen hundred hours. You have twenty-five minutes to save his neck, Mr. Thomas.'' He smiled down at the lawyer. ''Literally.''

''I quite understand, your honor.'' *You bastard.* He retrieved the box. ''Mr. Dore, I hand you this box, Defendant's Exhibit 1 for identification, and I ask you if you can further identify it.''

''Yes. It's a psi-enhancer—a psychic transmitter. It was developed by the research staff of Penal Systems, Incorporated, a company I own.''

''How does it work?''

''Well, nearly all of us have some measure of psychic powers. Basically this device enhances these powers. Call it psi if you like. Some of us have just a little psi. I'm one of those people. There are actually devices for measuring psi. On a scale of one to a hundred, I'm between eight and ten. Other people have a great deal. You're one of those, Mr. Thomas. You measure about ninety-eight.''

"You have called this a psi-enhancer. Just exactly how does it enhance psi?"

"I think I can explain that. Current research has pretty well established that psi stems from brain waves—alpha, beta, gamma, and a couple of others as yet not so clearly defined. This enhancer picks up those cranial radiations, amplifies them, focuses them, and rebroadcasts them according to the will of the subject. Transmission is apparently instantaneous, and the range is tremendous. Our experimenters have hit targets beyond the solar system. Jupiter is practically next door. The device is not perfect. There are occasional side effects, and there are risks. We are still working on these problems."

"Mr. Dore," said Thomas, "we have all heard Dr. Jarvis testify concerning a proposed seismic test. For this purpose, a nuclear device is presently sitting in a five-hundred-meter shaft on the other side of the moon. You are aware of that?"

"Yes."

Vulpin was on his feet. "Milord! Objection! What's this all about? First we have a mysterious black box, now we are rehashing Dr. Jarvis's seismic research program—all totally irrelevant. I move to strike the entire testimony of this witness!"

"Mr. Thomas?" queried Rile.

"It's all tied together, milord. We proceed in steps. First, we will use the black box, Defendant's Exhibit 1, to detonate Dr. Jarvis's seismic device. That will prove causation and the capability of the box. Secondly, and I state this for the record, the box has already been used to ignite Jupiter, and our forthcoming seismic detonation will prove this."

Vulpin threw up his hands. "Mad . . . mad . . ."

Rile was silent. He looked over at the wall holo. No activity. He turned back and studied Thomas thoughtfully. Thomas knew what the man was thinking: Rile was wondering if there was any truth to this fantastic scenario. If there was, Rile must stop the trial right there and then remove—*destroy*—the box. (Could it be done safely?) But none of this could be true. It just couldn't be. And he couldn't do anything that would suggest he believed, that he was uneasy . . . He said, "Go ahead, Mr. Thomas. Let's see what you can do."

(I wish I knew for sure myself, thought the lawyer.) He said, "Mr. Dore, I hand you now this black box, Defendant's Exhibit for identification D-1. It appears to have a hinged lid, which is presently closed. Will you open the box, please."

"Certainly." Dore folded the lid back.

"Now, would you please put it in operating condition. Explain what you are doing, for the record."

"Yes, first I pull out this pair of silver antennae. Next, I pull out this little cable. It has a terminal that can plug into a cranial insert."

Thomas took the cable end and faced the recording stenographer. "Let the record show that I have taken the cable terminus and that I am now connecting it to a cranial insert behind my left ear. Like so, Mr. Dore?"

"Exactly right."

"Now," continued Thomas, "I am fine-tuning these dials on the box. I have to focus . . . very precisely. Time check: nine minutes before five. I am now about to close the circuit. Following that, I will seem to black out for a few seconds. During that interval, I shall detonate Dr. Jarvis's bomb. I shall then 'return,' as it were. There may be a few moments of initial disorientation, but that should pass quickly. Time check, eight minutes before five."

He leaned against the dock railing and flipped the toggle. This time he knew exactly what to do.

Out . . . and there he was . . . looking it over. Just as Jarvis had said. At the bottom of a five-hundred-meter shaft, a lethal grapefruit, coated with C-4. You said well, Dr. Jarvis, and I hate to do this to you. But a great deal is at stake. Also, I'm going to improve on your technique just a bit. You get only fourteen percent yield because your C-4 doesn't blow all at once. Some goes off a few nanoseconds before the rest. The shock wave is ragged when it comes together in the Pu center. But I can blow it with perfect simultaneity, because I can stand stationary in time. We're going for one hundred percent yield, doctor, and we're going to do more than rattle the dome.

He enveloped the little sphere with his mind.

The shell of plasticized trinitrotoluene began to glow. And now he backed away. Quickly.

He was out, and back in court. He shook his head to clear his mind.

And now a familiar voice. It is Vulpin. "Move to strike! Silly . . . silly . . ."

Thomas exchanged glances with Michael Dore, then looked up toward the chancellor. "Emergency, milord! Will your lordship please order the Rotunda cleared!"

"And why?"

"Because the dome will come down in—" he looked at his watch—"six minutes and thirty seconds."

"I agree with Mr. Vulpin," declared Rile harshly. "You have tried to make a mockery of these proceedings, Mr. Thomas, and it is by no fault of your own that you have not succeeded. Indeed, perhaps you *have* succeeded. In any case I hold you in further contempt of court, this time on a criminal court."

Thomas shrugged. "Sorry for the inconvenience, milord. In any case, that completes the case for the defense."

"Rebuttal, Mr. Vulpin?"

"Nothing further, milord."

Just then a clerk dashed through the chancellor's back entrance and rushed breathlessly up onto the dais. He handed his lordship a piece of paper. Rile read it quickly, then once more, slowly, unbelieving.

Thomas chuckled, and whispered to Dore: "Looks like bad news from Maryland. It worked, and she's safe!"

"Oh, good show!" returned Dore. "We—"

CLANG . . . CLANG . . . CLANG . . .

It was all coming from the side wall—from the holo screen tuned to Arthur Clarke Station on Io. Red lights flashed in horrid synchronization with the clangor.

19
Io—II

Fair as the moon, clear as the sun, and terrible as an army with banners.
—*Song of Solomon*

Save for audio from the holo, the courtroom was silent. All faces turned and locked into that distant, eerie tableau.

The holo blurred. Boslow had dashed in, briefly obscuring the view of the gauge wall. He was tapping furiously at the Jovian temperature dials, surface and core. He paused a moment and rubbed his eyes. His paralyzed audience could see a shower of sweat droplets. He sat back heavily in his console chair.

Thomas looked at Dore. His client seemed suddenly sad, impassive.

In distant hell Boslow leaned slowly over the panel and pulled a switch. The bells and flashing lights stopped.

Just then another messenger ran up to the chancellor, waving a second note. Rile read it quickly, then began flailing away with his gavel. He soon realized that his courtroom was silent to begin with. He called out: "The observatory reports they see no change in Jupiter. The planet is not igniting." He flashed a savage grin at Thomas.

"He's wrong," whispered Dore. "It takes a while to show in the telescopes."

Back on the screen, Boslow turned his chair around and stared up at the camera. "There is some mistake," he declared hoarsely. "Jupiter is not igniting. I can prove it. We'll bring in an overhead visual. You can catch it here on the number two screen.'' He pointed toward a screen in the upper left hand corner of his console.

Don't do this, Boslow, Thomas moaned inwardly. It's bad enough, just *knowing* what's happening, and what must follow. Well, there it is, you've brought it in on the number two screen. You can sense the change. Faster and faster. A pulsing, swirling, in the pink and yellow planetary cloud belts. And here it comes. Wow! Swelling out like a hazy blustering balloon. Bigger and bigger. You want to try the observatory now, milord? And hey, what's that little white ball? Looks like Amalthea, one of the four tiny inner moons. That means J3 and Adrastea have already been gobbled up. J2's on the other side, a nice *hors d'oeuvre*. You're next, Amalthea. How far out now? That's very easy to determine, because your orbit lies one hundred and eighty-one thousand kilometers from Jupiter. So that means the lusty ball has swollen outward to that distance. And why swell? Because the internal heat is making the molecules dance. They move farther and farther apart. And they're not done yet, not by any means.

As Thomas watched, fascinated, a massive cloud roiled up around the speeding moonlet, and it vanished. Swallowed like a pill. God, that was fast! Ah, poor, poor Amalthea. Too too cruel, Jupiter, you brainless ingrate. Amalthea is the goat that nursed you when you were in infant god. She dies now by your violent hand. This is matricide. (What am I saying? *I* did this!)

Io, dearest and loveliest, you are next. Station, keeper, and all. But the other three Galileans will be safe, warm, habitable. A man dies on Io as the harbinger of civilizations to come on Europa, Ganymede, and Callisto. So be it.

Boslow looked up at the camera. He was saying something, over and over. "Help me . . . help me . . .''? wondered Thomas.

Everyone in the courtroom is now part of the horror of Boslow's face. For that matter, thought Thomas, so is everyone in comfortable Terran parlors, chained to their holos. There was something pure, spectral, crystalline in Boslow's consternation. It was like a mask of ancient Greek theater. It expressed one thing only, and that with devastating clarity.

Thomas could imagine what might be going on in the mind of the doomed engineer. No way to get away, no place to hide. Ah, he's pulling on his space suit. Is he going to make a break for it? Run for the dark side, where the monster didn't glower down from the overhead skies? Where everything would be cold, black, peaceful, serene? Forget it, Boslow. You'd never make it. Your ravenous guest is about to gulp down your entire moon, dark side and all.

Ah, what's that? Boslow lifts up a hinged floor plate. He'll try the cellar. That'll delay things a little. The engineer lifted up the hinged floor plate and carefully stepped down invisible stairs. The door clanged down above his head.

Thomas sighed. Burning is probably one of the nastier ways to die. Ask anybody. Ask Joan of Arc. Ask people trapped in a burning building. Ask animals in a forest fire. Ask those who didn't make it out of Pompeii and Herculaneum two thousand years ago.

It couldn't last much longer. The lawyer was certain that the delicate broadcasting electronics must yield any moment to the insatiable Jovian digestive juices. Yes, there it goes. First a scramble of whirling colors in the three-D panorama. Then solid black, white, and gray segments. Then nothing. The screen was dead. Probably, he thought, so was that poor devil in the cellar. He didn't want to think about him.

Oh hell. What could he or Dore have done or said that would have convinced the enemy this was going to happen? Probably nothing. It was written.

People in the room were beginning to talk again. The clerk was whispering something to the stenographer. The bailiff was talking to a couple of guards. It seemed to Thomas the sounds were an audio laminate of otherworldly murmurs. Something querulous, unbelieving, pleading, untranslatable.

Rile listened for a moment, then began to hammer at what seemed invisible insects crawling on his bench. "Silence!"

"Milord!" called Thomas.

Rile looked down at him in total hate. It occurred to Thomas that perhaps the chancellor ought to be at least a little bit grateful for the return to normal judicial procedures. But clearly, he wasn't. "Mr. Thomas?"

"Milord, based on Mr. Vulpin's own holo evidence, Jupiter has obviously ignited. I move the case be dismissed."

"Well, I don't know. The screen has blanked. We don't really know what's going on. I remind you, Mr. Thomas, I told you in the beginning I would not accept a holo transmission as evidence of ignition. I have to see it hanging there in the sky. Mr. Vulpin, may we have your views as to Mr. Thomas's motion?"

"I oppose the motion, milord. The holo transmission in any case must be regarded as incomplete. As your lordship so logically points out, we don't really know what's going on. The transmission was cut off, and we don't know how it all came out. Furthermore, the shots of Jupiter were not explained by expert testimony. Finally, the exhibition is simply an electronic copy of the actual scene. To admit this exhibition would be a clear violation of the best evidence rule."

Thomas started to remind Vulpin that this was the prosecutor's own evidence he was maligning, but then he decided to save his breath. He had to bear in mind that Rile's court was in a surrealistic juridical world, where some of the rules of evidence applied, some didn't, and all rules changed moment by moment. It was a sort of Wonderland that required exegesis by Lewis Carroll. Actually, in a way it was intriguing. In a moment of whimsy he decided to explore further. On into the tulgey wood! Might as well get it on the record. "While Dr. Boslow lived, he was your witness. Are you going to impeach your own witness?"

Vulpin shook his head in slow sorrow. "It's not a question of impeachment, Mr. Thomas. The statements of a dead man are simply not admissible. That's the Dead Man Rule. It's as old as Henry VI. You should know that."

"Then you admit that Jupiter killed him?"

Vulpin blinked, but recovered quickly. "Oh, now, I wouldn't go quite *that* far. Dead, Mr. Thomas? We don't have an actual flesh-and-blood witness in court here who saw him die. And it must follow we don't know whether Jupiter killed him."

Curiouser and curiouser.

"But he was *about* to die? That's why he went down into the cellar? Surely you will agree that that act, per se, was a dying declaration, and an admission of imminent death? Or do you think he was going down into the wine cellar in his space suit to select something for supper?"

"Well, now that's a thought, isn't it. It would have been a bit early for supper, but you'll recall it was getting warm, and it would take time to chill the wine properly."

He's totally mad, thought Thomas. And yet it all has a remarkable internal consistency. He said: "Will the learned prosecutor stipulate that the holo transmission system was destroyed by Jupiter?"

"No, certainly not. I was ready to terminate the broadcast in any event."

"How about Dr. Boslow's exclamations of alarm. Will you admit those as part of the *res gestae*?"

"Again, no. The audio was going bad about that time. Who knows what he was saying?"

Thomas looked around the courtroom slowly.

Rile said sharply, "What are you doing, Mr. Thomas?"

He wanted to say, looking for the Mad Hatter, the White Rabbit, the Dormouse . . . He said, "Oh, sorry, milord. Just waiting for your lordship to rule on my motion to dismiss."

"I'm going to rule. I will say at the outset that both counsel, in oral argument, have analyzed the pros and cons thoroughly, so that I can come immediately to the point and give a bench ruling.

"The motion is denied. The court will adhere to our original requirement, namely that the new sun must be visible in the sky. A few incomprehensible blurs on a holo screen hardly qualify, Mr. Thomas."

"But—your honor could call the observatory!"

"Sit down, Mr. Thomas. These proceedings are closed."

As he resumed his seat Dore handed him a note. "From Wright. It just came in on the computer: 'Rile seventy percent.' "

"That makes him the head honcho of the syndicate," whispered the lawyer. "And it explains just about everything. But he's too late. It doesn't matter anymore." He looked up at the wall clock. Two minutes to five.

Rile swiveled his high-backed chair and faced the jury. "Gentlemen. The defendant Mr. Michael Dore has been indicted for the crime of conspiracy to prevent the completion of that endeavor known as the Lamplighter Project. Associated with this count are lesser charges of embezzlement, fraud, and theft. These lesser offenses merge into the basic offense, conspiracy, which under our lunar statutes, is equivalent to treason, a capital offense. The defendant promised to ignite Jupiter by five o'clock this afternoon. It is now almost five o'clock.

"Proof of treason requires two witnesses. You have heard three nuclear experts testify that the defendant cannot ignite Jupiter. You have heard wild claims that Jupiter has in fact ignited. These claims have little probative value. The only sure proof of ignition is to see Jupiter, as a new sun, actually hanging in the overhead skies." He paused and closed his eyes as if in pleasant introspective thought. "If you agree with any two of the three prosecution experts, you must find that the defendant is guilty of a breach of an inviolate undertaking to the Federation. Such breach of trust is treason, and the penalty is death. You will now retire, select your foreman, and reach a verdict."

Where oh where is that rumble, thought Thomas. Or a rattle. Or just a tingle in my toes.

The foremost juryman stood up. Thomas recognized Kudder. "Your honor, I'm the foreman. They elected me at lunchtime. We don't need to retire. We've already reached a verdict."

20
Sentence First, Verdict After

Demoniac frenzy, moping melancholy,
And moonstruck madness.
    —John Milton, Paradise Lost

Interesting, thought Thomas. They haven't even taken a vote.

And I think I feel something. A very nice vibration in the floor.

"And what is your verdict, Mr. Foreman?" Rile's question dripped with honey. He removed his wig and placed the black cap on his head.

Now just one computer-pickin' minute, thought Thomas. You're not supposed to put on the black cap until you hear the guilty verdict. Even *here!* Except that . . . actually he's following the Wonderland script verbatim: Sentence first—verdict afterwards. So this is all quite proper. And soon we'll all wake up, with a pack of cards flying about our faces.

And here comes the verdict.

"Guilty, your honor."

Surprise, surprise, thought the lawyer.

"Will the defendant rise?" commanded Rile.

Dore got to his feet. "Just seconds now," he whispered to Thomas.

"This court," boomed Rile, "declares that you have had a fair and impartial trial on the charge of treason and that you have been found guilty by a fair and impartial jury of your peers. Michael Dore, have you anything to say before I pronounce sentence?"

"Nothing," said the prisoner. "All is now said. All is now done."

Rile didn't try to understand. "The prisoner having been given the opportunity to speak, I pronounce sentence. Michael Dore, I sentence you to death. Your evil corpus is to be taken immediately from this room, and it will be given to the blade, and your head will be severed from your body. May God have mercy on your soul. The guards will now escort you to the Rotunda."

As he finished his declaration, the lord chancellor looked up. The ceiling luminex panels were flickering.

No matter. Justice gallops.

Four burly uniformed guards brushed aside a loudly protesting Thomas and began twisting Dore's hands behind his back to handcuff him. But they were having trouble, because the floor was shaking. One guard was suddenly sick. Making gasping gurgling sounds, he turned aside and leaned on the prosecutor's table. Vulpin backed away.

At that moment several other things happened of an even more puzzling nature. The courtroom was filled with a clanging roar, as though all Lunaplex had turned into a monster bell.

The lights went out.

Thomas seemed to remember that the safety irises were operative by emergency power. Some air would be lost, but then the irises would close. He smiled happily, and he waited.

Here it came. He followed the architectural catastrophe in the Rotunda with his ears. It really surprised him how long it took for the dome to disintegrate. It didn't collapse all at once. It sounded as though it were tumbling down a block or two at a time. He wanted to go outside and watch, but of course that was out of the question. Was it falling in the reverse order in which it had been built, with the crest dropping first? Probably no way to know. Makes a marvelous crescendo, though. And what's that roar? Ah, of course, air swooshing out through the great hole left by the fallen dome, into the vacuum of the lunar sky.

And wow! Look at that red glare, coming in from the Rotunda, right into the courtroom! Fire? Yes! The fires of

Jupiter! The new sun, shining bountifully in the open sky. Oh beautiful crimson glare! thought Thomas. He looked happily up toward the bemused chancellor. A clear and flagrant trespass, Rile. Outrageous contempt of court! Are you going to stand for this? Couldn't we have at least a per curiam rebuke, milord? Tell it to go away?

But the lord chancellor seemed disinclined to issue any orders or make any rulings. He sat there at the bench, immobile, visible only because of flickering red outlines. The bloated face opened and closed, opened and closed. Finally sounds began to come out of the face. The man shrieked something unintelligible, stumbled down from the dais, and hurtled past tables and bar and down the courtroom aisle toward the closing exit iris. The red glare was temporarily dimmed by interposition of the running man, but Thomas could see everything.

Rile stooped before the closed iris, peering through the little window of hardened glass in the very center. The ambiguous red glow from outside waved in and around the man's face, like flowering fires from some mythic Valhalla burning, and forever changing the fate of the world.

Quentin Thomas studied the creature at the iris for a moment, and he thought back to an incident in an undergraduate chemistry course. Organic 21. He had been standing just inside the swinging doors of the lab. At a bench somewhere behind him a liter of ether ignited. The expanding gases had blown him head over heels through the door, like a pellet through a dart gun. He had landed on his back halfway down the corridor.

In his mind he measured the distance from iris to guillotine. It would work.

But then he paused. Did he need to do this terrible thing? The great farce was all over. Or was it? As long as Rile lived, were he, Dore, Nadys safe? And that scene in Rile's chambers, blowing his nose on . . . Rile the desecrator . . . Oh, damn you forever!

The lawyer searched out the iris circuitry, imbedded in the door side. It was plainly laid out, and closing the circuit and reactivating the iris was no problem.

Martin Rile, thought Quentin Thomas, you have murdered, and would murder again, and I now pronounce sentence.

The iris blades began to spin back into their receptacles. At first, the great rush of air simply pinned the jurist against the central iris orifice. He screamed, but it got him nothing. Then, as the blades continued their inexorable withdrawal, there was a mighty whoomp, and Lord Chancellor Martin Rile was blown out into the semi-vacuum of the Rotunda. Throughout his perilous low-gravity flight he remained in Thomas's line of sight. The lawyer caught a last glimpse of a terrified red-lit face, staring up toward the miraculous nemesis sun.

The scant courtroom audience had a marvelous if momentary view of events in the Rotunda.

Rile landed backwards on the guillotine platform. Three button-terminated cables flung out from nowhere and lashed at the short man's face. He grabbed at all three. The blade went up, then flashed down.

The lawyer thought of crazy lines from *Through the Looking-Glass* ". . . The vorpal blade went snicker-snack . . ."

And now pale blue luminars began shining down from the courtroom ceiling. Emergency power was coming on, Thomas surmised. By the newly available light he noted activity in the jury box.

The lawyer leaped at Dore and pulled him to the floor just as a thin red light stabbed across the defense table.

"Kudder's got a laser," whispered Thomas. "Stay down."

"Can you fix it?"

"Yes, I think so. Well, look at *that*." They both looked over at the prosecutor. A dark blot was spreading over the left side of Vulpin's chest. For a few seconds the champion of the people just stood there, sincere in his total astonishment. Then he crumpled, and he was dead before he hit the floor.

"We ducked, and he got it," explained Thomas. "We can get up now."

As they clambered to their feet, a second ray of light sprayed at them.

"It's harmless," explained the lawyer. "The beam is no

longer homogeneous—just plain white light. I jammed his synchronizer.''

The erstwhile jury foreman yelled something unpleasant and threw the useless weapon at them. It clattered along the table and fell to the floor. The man leaped over the jury railing and ran toward the iris, which Thomas obligingly opened again. Kudder sailed outward on a fine blast of air.

''This is getting monotonous,'' muttered the lawyer.

''Air pressure will equalize in another couple of minutes,'' observed his client philosophically. ''Then you'll lose your job as doorman.''

''Kudder'll get away.''

''Not really. Where can he go? The cops will eventually figure out who the bad guys are. They'll pick him up.''

As they waited, a final merciful clutch of blocks fell over the scene outside, and then the courtroom iris opened once more, this time to stay.

Together, lawyer and client rushed down the center aisle and out into the near-lunar landscape that had once been the garden spot of Lunaplex. They picked their way through rubble and dust curtains.

Poised carefully amid tumbled basalt masonry, they stared down at the face in the basket. The sparse hair stood straight out from the scalp, as though from a strong electrostatic charge. But the look on the dead face convinced them that such was not the cause. The wide eyes were filled with a weird blend of awe and terror. Thomas knelt down to close the eyes. As he did this, he had a curious prickling thought. Had *he* accomplished this miracle of timing, air blast, and body velocity? Or was this (as some might contend) the act of an intervening (interfering?) God. Forget it, Thomas, he told himself; too deep for you.

''Quentin . . .'' Dore was tapping him on the shoulder. As he got up, his client pointed to a second body, partially hidden in the rubble. A single massive block had crushed the head.

Thomas suddenly felt faint. He had caused this. He had no qualms about Rile. But this second, accidental corpse! Murder? Had he done murder?

''Relax, dear chap. It's Kudder. The people are grateful

to you. You saved them the expense of a long trial.''

''Kudder?'' Rile, Vulpin, Kudder. Truly a *dies irae*—day of rage. But let this be the end of it.

At this instant he sensed a near-soundless rumbling, coming as though from sublunar depths. He and Dore exchanged wondering glances. *Now* what?

They were answered immediately.

The jets of the nearby French fountain burst into noisy life.

''*Water!*'' shouted Thomas, over the howl of the spray. ''Real *water*! We opened up a fissure right below us!''

Dore grinned back at him, then pointed. Only two of the streams met overhead. The third spigot had been knocked awry by falling debris. It was spraying across the pool and onto the guillotine. The machine and the two-piece lord chancellor were being liberally laved by waters sparkling red in the light of that new distant sun.

Thomas pointed at the bronze plaque affixed to the misjointed jet: *Purgaro*. I purify.

Let it be so.

''Where does it drain to?'' wondered Dore.

''Ultimately to general waste, I suppose.''

Another commotion. They were nearly knocked down by a figure dashing past. The apparition paused a moment before the pool, now beginning to fill, and then he (they now recognized Dr. Jarvis, of the Geologic Survey) held his arms up in a great victorious thrust and began to speak in tongues.

''What's he saying?'' Dore asked mildly.

''I caught 'apophyllite,' 'brucite,' 'colemanite.' I think he's reciting all lunar minerals that contain water of crystallization. It's rather a long list. When he gets to 'zoisite,' I wonder if he will repeat.''

They watched the survey director as he ripped off shoes, jacket, trousers, shirt, and tossed them away. Then underwear, socks . . . everything. And then he was in the pool, dancing, screaming, pirouetting. His spectacles dangled precariously from one ear.

''Is he happy?'' asked Dore.

''Yes, I think so,'' said the lawyer. In a lunarlike way, he added to himself. He let the thought meander on. On

Earth, people under lunar influence are called lunatics. *A fortiori*, what do they become when they *live* here?

"Gentlemen . . ." He looked around. The Damage Control crew had arrived with vans and sweepers, stretchers, and body bags. The foreman was politely urging everyone to leave.

That was fine with him. He wanted to call Nadys. If he could just hear her voice, he thought he could reenter the real world.

He reached into his pocket, pulled out a couple of coins, and tossed them into the frothing pool.

And so back to A-A.

Several hours later, when they were finally able to return to the Rotunda, they surveyed the scene of former catastrophe.

The fountain was now working beautifully. The three jets were united overhead at the proper point. Dr. Jarvis, now fully clad, was sitting silently on the pool edge, with his trousered legs dangling in the water. Madame de Maintenon would have approved, decided Thomas.

All the clutter of fallen stones had been hauled away. There was no sign of corpse or guillotine. The terrazo plaza flooring had been scrubbed and polished. The great circular hole overhead had been temporarily sealed off with a hemisphere of thick polyolefin.

"They got what they wanted," said Thomas. "Those three."

"And what might that be?" asked Michael Dore.

"Peace Eternal."

"*Did* they now?"

There was something chilling in Dore's question that made the lawyer decide not to carry the matter further. He might find out who Michael-who-is-like-God Dore was. And he was not sure he really wanted to know.

21
Moon-borne Melodies

Yet we'll go no more a-roving
By the light of the moon.
  —*George Noel Gordon, Lord Byron,*
    "So We'll Go No More A-Roving."

They had been in flight aboard Dore's Lamplighter courier ship for four hours when Quentin Thomas finally got through to Nadys.

She had returned to her apartment. She had had much to say, and he was glad that he was alone in the tiny message booth while she said it. First, there was the matter of leaving the planet without a word.

"I didn't know I was going. They said they would tell you. Didn't they tell you?"

His defense was halfhearted and unconvincing. He didn't care. He couldn't take his eyes off her flickering image in the two-D screen. Even with the flawed transmission her eyes seemed soft and black. From those eyes he reconstructed his beloved in all her beauty and complexity, the way an archeologist reconstructs a civilization from a pottery shard. He saw her complete, along a time line. He saw a scrawny little girl in pigtails, then a leggy adolescent. Then his wife, mother of his children. Middle age. Then old and wrinkled and lovelier than ever. It stopped there, presumably because he would predecease her. Was it all his imagination? It must be, because now he could smell her.

She was talking to him. "Yes, they told me you'd be gone a few days. But not where or why. I had to find that out from the holos. It was embarrassing. I couldn't explain anything to my acquaintances.''

He was curious. ''How did it come out on holo? How did I look?''

''Not so good. Everything you did or said, they objected to. You got overruled a lot.''

''Yeah.''

''We missed most of the afternoon session.''

''How's that?''

''Wasn't it on the news? No, I guess not. Just local stuff. All the Patuxent Haven fire alarms went off. The noise was scary. About a million sprinklers came on, right in our private rooms. Everybody got soaked. We had to run out on the lawns. You should have been able to hear the screams all the way to the moon. About ten fire crews came, but they couldn't find anything. They handed out blankets. You didn't hear about it?''

''Not sure. There might have been some kind of report. We were pretty busy here.''

''Busy? Oh, you mean about the dome collapse?''

''Well, yeah, that . . .''

''We heard the judge ran out into it and got killed. Too bad. He was so cute and roly-poly.''

Thomas sighed. ''He was going out to look at Jupiter.''

''The planet? Oh, of course. It exploded, or something.''

''So they say.'' He paused. Would he ever attempt to explain it all to her? Maybe, someday. Right now, though, it simply wasn't important. It was time for the question. ''Nadys?''

''I never finished the retreat,'' she interposed. ''So don't ask. Not just yet.''

''I'm not asking. I'm telling you. We will be married the day after I return.''

''That's much too soon. We have to get the invitations printed. We have to draw up lists. We have to make arrangements with the church. Wedding rehearsals. Bridal showers. I need two months.''

''One month. And that's it.''

''Well, all right.''

* * *

He returned to Dore's private compartment and strapped in once more.

He knew that the great man was watching him, speculating, trying to guess the answer to the question he was about to ask the lawyer.

Dore cleared his throat. "Much remains to be done, Quentin. Those Jovian moons have to be prepared for mass immigrations. We have a skeleton organization in place, but we're going to have to face an exponential administrative expansion. I'll need a deputy director. Good pay. Perks, including predated stock options. We opened at nine hundred and five this morning. You'll be an automatic millionaire. How about it?" He waited. "Quentin?"

"I'm thinking."

"Oh. Of course. Go ahead."

Money. *That*, he thought, would certainly be nice. Anyone who has ever been hungry loves money. And millionaire? He could not visualize that kind of money. It lay somewhere way over the horizon.

BUT—

If he signed on with Dore he would thereafter see very little of Nadys. What kind of life was that? He wondered if she would be waiting for him at the Oldcolumbia Spaceport. And he was also thinking of several other things. Of psi, for instance. Yes, a lot about psi.

Psi existed. And because a machine could transmit that psi over unimaginable distances, Jupiter hung red in the skies. That was just the start. There were other solar systems. Even other galaxies. He could reach out to all of them. God almighty. Where was the end? *Was* there an end?

He didn't really care. He refused to be some sort of superman. He was just a plain human being. "Be not afraid of greatness: some are born great, some achieve greatness, and some have greatness thrust upon them." *Twelfth Night*. He wasn't afraid of it. That wasn't the problem. Greatness simply didn't interest him. Of course, some of it he was stuck with—in his role as winning counsel in the case of the century. All that had been on worldwide casts, and he couldn't escape it. But at least nobody (Dore always excepted) knew he'd blown Jupiter or the great dome. All was not lost. He could still return to the safe, sane, comfortable life of a patent lawyer. (Did he still have his old job at Laurence, Gottlieb? And what would Mr. Gottlieb say when he learned the guillotine had been destroyed? Could they claim a tax loss? Michael Dore had a lot of fence-mending to do.)

No.

He had made his decision, and Dore was entitled to know that decision. He said, "I'm grateful, Mike. I'll never forget the offer. But I don't think I'll be any good in administration. I'm just a hack lawyer. And I guess that's what I'll always be."

Dore smiled. "Whatever you say, Quentin. If you change your mind, let me know. We'll always have room for you." From somewhere he pulled out his keyboard and riffed a casual chord.

Thomas relaxed and turned back to his own thoughts.

What now?

Perhaps things would never get back to normal. On the other hand, he was still a lawyer, and now that this little *entr'act* was over, he had a duty to PSI, which was, after all, his retaining client, regardless of Dore's ultimate ownership. PSI owned the psi-enhancer, and he had to get their decision as to whether they wanted to keep the circuitry a trade secret, or whether they wanted to try to patent it. He'd have to be ready with all the pros and cons. Did it in fact involve patentable subject matter? You can't patent a scientific principle per se, or a law of nature, or a mental act, or (generally speaking) a machine that required a mental act to function. That had been settled for ages. He tried to think back to the old cases. Would the enhancer fall within the Musgrave Exception? Would he have to provide and demonstrate a model under Rule 92? And perhaps the most crucial factor of all was the impact of the Nuclear Statutes. The Patent Office was trigger-happy about putting alleged nuclear cases under secrecy order. Mr. Gottlieb had once filed a simple phosphate fertilizer application. It had been placed under secrecy order, because, explained the examiner, everybody knew Florida phosphate contained traces of uranium. That was five years ago, and the order was still under appeal. And even if the P.O. didn't act initially, the government could require the secrecy order; and not only that, they could seize the application by eminent domain. And maybe him along with it! Crazy, unexpected things could happen. Somebody else would have to decide. Wright? No, not Wright. The inventor(s)? And who was he/they? Dore, sole.

Dore had been sitting there, playing his keyboard, and probably simultaneously reading him. What had the musician been playing? Mozart's Symphony Number 40, the great Jupiter. Fugue finale. Quite *apropos*.

"I think we should try to patent it," said Dore. He didn't miss a note.

"Yes." He thought about that. It would be a chancy thing, and he'd have to get it in front of a friendly examiner. Was there any way to get it to Nadys? After all, she'd be doing business as usual at the Patent Office for at least another month. After they were married, even if she continued to work, she wouldn't be able to handle his cases anymore. Conflict of interest.

He tried to chart a course for the application through the Patent Office to her desk. After recording in the Application Branch it would go to the Classification Division. A classification examiner would look it over and pick out the broadest claim. Then he would send it to the group handling the subject matter covered in that claim. So the attorney had considerable control over where his case wound up. It all depended on how he worded the main claim. At the outset he had to decide on language that would exclude the chemical groups. Group 110, for example, took the cases on Fuel and Igniting Devices. He couldn't mention anything like that. If that was Scylla, then Charybdis was the Mechanical Groups. In that category Group 340 examined heat-generating devices, and he'd have to be careful not to use words like that.

So, on to Nadys, in the Electrical Groups, specifically Group 220, Special Laws: Nuclear Reactors, Radioactivity, and Seismic Exploration. All he had to do was avoid words like nuclear and radioactive, and stick to words like seismic exploration.

From some other universe he noted that Dore had shifted from Mozart to Saint-Saens. Something from *Samson et Dalila: Mon coeur s' oeuvre à ta voix* . . . Dore, he thought, you are pretty damn intrusive. But now back to the filing strategy.

He would compose a beautiful main claim, something rhythmic. A claim just for her. Here we go.

1. De*vice* for *seis*mic *explora*tion . . .

(Ah, nice iambic tetrameter. She'll love that. Now, let's see. She's a sucker for dactyls. Let's work in a bit of dactyl.)

with a re*cep*tor for *cranial waves, means* for en*han*cing the *strength* of the *waves* . . .

Oh, it was *flowing*! Keats or Shelley or Byron could not have improved on it. He branched out. He elaborated. He worked rare, bizarre rhythm forms into the lines of the claim. His mind danced.

> *Now trochee is tricky*
> *And spondee is sticky*
> *And anapest's a mess!*
> *But I'll entrance her with amphimacer*
> *And a dash of diaeresis.*

Oh, he could handle any of them, all of them. In the same claim, even! To show his complete mastery of the medium, he wound up the claim with a line of blank verse:

. . . thereby to effect alteration in a remote environment.

(It all trembled between total clarity and total incomprehensibility: a sure sign of claim-drafting genius.)

Quentin Thomas was tremendously satisfied with himself. He had finally written the perfect claim. He fantasized. Nadys would allow it on her first action. He'd hop over to Crystal Plaza, and they would meet in his room at the Marriott to discuss it.

Vaguely, he noted that his client had moved into the great

love duet from *Tristan und Isolde*. *Oh sink hernieder, Nacht der Liebe* . . . "Descend upon us, night of love . . ."

Thomas started to ask Dore to mind his own business. Instead he said, "You never doubted. Why? Could you have taken over if I had failed?"

"No, I couldn't. You had to do it."

"But why were you so confident?"

"It's my type of psi. I have prescient flashes. I saw you and me on my return ship, a Lamplighter courier."

"That's why I had a one-way ticket?"

"Yes. I couldn't waste Lamplighter money, could I? That would be embezzlement."

"Treason," said Thomas.

"Right. A capital offense!"

ARTHUR C. CLARKE'S VENUS PRIME™

by Paul Preuss

VOLUME 1: BREAKING STRAIN   75344-8/$3.95 US/$4.95 CAN
Her code name is Sparta. Her beauty veils a mysterious past and
abilities of superhuman dimension, the product of advanced
biotechnology.

VOLUME 2: MAELSTROM   75345-6/$3.95 US/$4.95 CAN
When a team of scientists is trapped in the gaseous inferno of
Venus, Sparta must risk her life to save them.

VOLUME 3: HIDE AND SEEK   75346-4/$3.95 US/$4.95 CAN
When the theft of an alien artifact, evidence of extraterrestrial
life, leads to two murders, Sparta must risk her life and identity
to solve the case.

VOLUME 4: THE MEDUSA ENCOUNTER
                                    75348-0/$3.95 US/$4.95 CAN
Sparta's recovery from her last mission is interrupted as she sets
out on an interplanetary investigation of her host, the Space
Board.

VOLUME 5: THE DIAMOND MOON
                                    75349-9/$3.95 US/$4.95 CAN
Sparta's mission is to monitor the exploration of Jupiter's moon,
Amalthea, by the renowned Professor J.Q.R. Forester.

**Each volume features a special technical infopak,
including blueprints of the structures of *Venus Prime***

PRESENTING THE ADVENTURES OF

BY HARRY HARRISON

BILL, THE GALACTIC HERO

00395-3/$3.95 US/$4.95 Can

He was just an ordinary guy named Bill, a fertilizer operator from a planet of farmers. Then a recruiting robot shanghaied him with knockout drops, and he came to in deep space, aboard the Empire warship *Christine Keeler*

BILL, THE GALACTIC HERO: THE PLANET OF ROBOT SLAVES
75661-7/$3.95 US/$4.95 Can

BILL, THE GALACTIC HERO: ON THE PLANET OF BOTTLED BRAINS
75662-5/$3.95 US/$4.95 Can
(co-authored by Robert Sheckley)

BILL, THE GALACTIC HERO: ON THE PLANET OF TASTELESS PLEASURE
75664-1/$3.95 US/$4.95 Can
(co-authored by David Bischoff)

BILL, THE GALACTIC HERO: ON THE PLANET OF ZOMBIE VAMPIRES
75665-X/$3.95 US/$4.95 Can
(co-authored by Jack C. Haldeman II)

In the bestselling tradition of
The Hitchhiker's Guide to the Galaxy™

ENTER THE
INFOCOM™ UNIVERSE

THE LOST CITY OF ZORK
Robin W. Bailey
75389-8/$4.50 US/$5.50 CAN

THE ZORK CHRONICLES
George Alec Effinger
75388-X/$4.50 US/$5.50 CAN

STATIONFALL
Arthur Byron Cover
75387-1/$3.95 US/$4.95 CAN

ENCHANTER
Robin W. Bailey
75386-3/$3.95 US/$4.95 CAN

WISHBRINGER
Craig Shaw Gardner
75385-5/$3.95 US/$4.95 CAN

PLANETFALL
Arthur Byron Cover
75384-7/$3.95 US/$4.95 CAN